P9-DCJ-966

Claire glanced over her shoulder and caught him staring.

A perfectly arched brow lifted. "Are you coming?"

Devin had no idea where she was leading him, but it didn't matter—he would follow wherever she wanted to go.

It turned out she was only leading him as far as the tack room so that he could pick a saddle.

"Ready?" she asked.

He nodded and reached up for the saddle horn, ready to mount the bay stallion she'd assigned to him.

"Wait." She looped the reins in her hand around a fence post, then breached the distance between them and lifted her hand to his tie. "You're a little overdressed for where we're going."

He swallowed as her fingers—long and slender, with neatly trimmed and unpainted nails—loosened the knot at his throat. Then she tugged on one end, pulling the tie free from his collar, and moved to release the top button.

Her movements were brisk and impersonal, and at the same time, there was something incredibly intimate about her actions. She paused, as if only now realizing the same thing.

Her fingertips rested lightly on the placket of his shirt as she lifted her eyes to his.

The air between them crackled with electricity.

Dear Reader,

No more men; no more heartbreak.

That's Claire Lamontagne's mantra when she returns to her hometown of Haven, Nevada, after a decade away. And it's a simple enough rule to follow because she's too busy working on her ranch to spare any time for romance.

Then she hires Devin Blake to build a website for Twilight Valley—a horse-rescue facility—and discovers that there's so much more to the self-proclaimed computer nerd than meets the eye. Devin is sweet and charming, and his kisses curl her toes inside her boots—but Claire's heart remains wary.

It's going to take time and patience to convince this cowgirl to take a chance on love. Thankfully Devin's got plenty of both, along with a surprising secret of his own.

I've always enjoyed breaking gender stereotypes in real life and in my stories. I bought my niece her first Barbie, but I also bought her a Tonka truck, because I wanted her to know that there were options.

For this trip to Haven, Nevada, I thought it would be interesting to mix things up a little with the heroine being the rancher and the hero being the one who needs to learn a few lessons in love.

I hope you have as much fun reading *Captivated by the Cowgirl* as I had writing it! If you have any thoughts about Claire and Devin's story that you'd like to share, please visit me at Facebook.com/brenda.harlen or find me on Twitter @brendaharlen. And to keep up-to-date on new Match Made in Haven books and exclusive news, check out my website, brendaharlen.com.

Happy reading!

xo *Brenda*

Captivated
by the Cowgirl

——

BRENDA HARLEN

If you purchased this book without a cover you should be aware
that this book is stolen property. It was reported as "unsold and
destroyed" to the publisher, and neither the author nor the
publisher has received any payment for this "stripped book."

HARLEQUIN®
SPECIAL
EDITION™

Recycling programs
for this product may
not exist in your area.

ISBN-13: 978-1-335-40847-1

Captivated by the Cowgirl

Copyright © 2022 by Brenda Harlen

All rights reserved. No part of this book may be used or reproduced in
any manner whatsoever without written permission except in the case of
brief quotations embodied in critical articles and reviews.

This is a work of fiction. Names, characters, places and incidents
are either the product of the author's imagination or are used fictitiously.
Any resemblance to actual persons, living or dead, businesses,
companies, events or locales is entirely coincidental.

For questions and comments about the quality of this book,
please contact us at CustomerService@Harlequin.com.

Harlequin Enterprises ULC
22 Adelaide St. West, 41st Floor
Toronto, Ontario M5H 4E3, Canada
www.Harlequin.com

Printed in U.S.A.

Brenda Harlen is a former attorney who once had the privilege of appearing before the Supreme Court of Canada. The practice of law taught her a lot about the world and reinforced her determination to become a writer—because in fiction, she could promise a happy ending! Now she is an award-winning, RITA® Award–nominated, nationally bestselling author of more than fifty titles for Harlequin. You can keep up-to-date with Brenda on Facebook and Twitter, or through her website, brendaharlen.com.

Books by Brenda Harlen

Harlequin Special Edition

Match Made in Haven

Double Duty for the Cowboy
One Night with the Cowboy
A Chance for the Rancher
The Marine's Road Home
Meet Me Under the Mistletoe
The Rancher's Promise
The Chef's Surprise Baby
Captivated by the Cowgirl

Montana Mavericks:
The Real Cowboys of Bronco Heights

Dreaming of a Christmas Cowboy

Montana Mavericks: What Happened to Beatrix?

A Cowboy's Christmas Carol

Montana Mavericks: Six Brides for Six Brothers

Maverick Christmas Surprise

Montana Mavericks: The Lonelyhearts Ranch

Bring Me a Maverick for Christmas!

Visit the Author Profile page
at Harlequin.com for more titles.

This book is dedicated with love to Ryan, my in-house tech support and go-to source for gaming information.

The good stuff is all his; any errors are my own.

Chapter One

Devin Blake hated being interrupted when he was in the zone, which was why no one he knew ever showed up at his door without calling first—at least not more than once. So when the doorbell rang late on a Monday afternoon in early May, he ignored it.

Then it rang again.

And again.

Muttering with frustration, he tapped the screen of his phone, sitting on his desk beside his keyboard, and opened the security camera app to see if he could identify the person responsible for the disruption. If it was a courier, there was going to be hell to pay, because he'd given signature releases to all local delivery companies to ensure that he wouldn't be pulled away from his work for anything as mundane as signing for a package.

An image filled the screen, his jaw dropped and—for just a moment—he actually forgot what he was supposed to be doing and just stared.

Because his visitor was…stunning.

Loose waves of long blond hair framed a delicate heart-shaped face. Her eyes, dark green with ridiculously long lashes, dropped to glance at the watch—or maybe it was a fitness band—on her wrist. She wore a white scoop-neck top with little cap sleeves tucked into a slim-fitting skirt with wedge-heeled sandals on her feet.

Stunning but lost, he decided.

And persistent, he added to the assessment, as she reached forward to ring the bell again.

With a weary sigh—and perhaps a little bit of anticipation—he rose from his desk and made his way from his home office, through the living room to the front door.

"Oh, hi." Her smile was bright, her tone friendly. "I was beginning to think you weren't home. Or that I'd maybe put the wrong day or time in my calendar."

He should say something—anything—but his tongue was suddenly tied in knots.

"You're Devin, right?" she prompted, when he remained silent.

He nodded.

So much for his theory that she was in the wrong place, but he still didn't know who she was or why she was looking for him.

"I'm Claire," she said now, answering the first of his unspoken questions. "Claire Lamontagne."

The name was vaguely familiar, as if he should know who she was but his mind failed to make a connection. He automatically accepted her proffered hand. Though it looked slender, even delicate, her grip was firm, and he felt a jolt of something electric pass between them.

He suspected that she'd felt it, too, because she quickly pulled her hand away even as she smiled again.

"When you talk to Sarah, can you tell her that I was here at four?"

He assumed she was referring to Sarah Stafford, which suggested that Claire was a friend of his cousin— but it still didn't explain this woman's presence at his door.

"She thinks there's something in my DNA that makes it impossible for me to ever be on time, but I am today," Claire continued. "Of course, I set three alerts on my phone to ensure I wouldn't be late, but I'm here and ready to get started."

She paused to catch a breath, giving him a chance to untangle his tongue and ask, "Started with what?"

Delicately arched brows drew together over those deep green eyes. "The website for Twilight Valley. I was so focused on getting everything ready and then taking care of the horses, I didn't even think about a website, but Sarah assured me that you're a whiz at computer stuff and could get one set up for me in no time."

Finally, the pieces clicked into place for him.

"You're the friend with the horse rescue," he said, as vague memories of a recent conversation with his cousin nudged at his mind.

"It's a rehabilitation and retirement facility," Claire told him.

"Right."

The furrow between those brows deepened. "Do I have the wrong day for our meeting?"

He could say yes and maybe save face, but then she might end up feeling as foolish as he did right now. Instead, he answered truthfully.

"I don't know," he admitted.

Because if Sarah had mentioned a specific date and time for a meeting with her friend, he had no memory of it, and there had been no commitments noted in his electronic calendar.

"But I obviously caught you in the middle of something," Claire realized.

"Yeah. I'm trying to build an extra layer of security for—" He caught the blank look on her face and quickly cut himself off. "Well, I'm sure you're not interested in firewall design."

"I might be, if I had the slightest clue what you were talking about," she told him.

"So I'll just say that yes, I was in the middle of something."

And it was critical work that he really needed to get back to, but at the moment, he was completely spellbound by his cousin's friend.

Of course, he was neither foolish nor foolhardy enough to think that a woman who looked like Claire Lamontagne would ever be interested in a guy like him. The only reason she was at his door was that she wanted a website built, and apparently holding dual degrees in software engineering and computer science qualified him for that.

Claire waited a beat, as if expecting Devin to say something else, but the power of speech eluded him again.

"Why don't we reschedule our meeting then?" she finally suggested.

He nodded, grateful that she'd managed to come up with an admittedly obvious solution to the problem. "That would be good."

She offered him another of those smiles that took his breath away. "Tell me what works for you."

"Thursday?" he suggested.

"Are you telling me or asking me?" She sounded amused.

Of course she was amused—because he was acting like an imbecile.

Because he was a genius with computers and an idiot with women.

"Um."

Yeah, that single syllable wasn't going to do anything to improve her opinion of him. Nothing was as effective as incomplete words and incomprehensible sounds to make an intelligent man sound like a blathering fool.

He tore his gaze from her face to check the calendar app on his phone.

"Thursday works for me," he said. A statement, not a question this time. "I've got a meeting at Blake Mining in the morning, but I should be done by ten."

He ventured another glance in her direction, and

somehow managed not to stumble over his words as he added, "For sure no later than eleven."

"Here's an idea—why don't you come by Twilight Valley when you're done? Whether it's eleven or twelve or even later, I'll be there."

"I can do that," he agreed, adding the meeting to his calendar to ensure he wouldn't forget the next time.

But as he lifted his hand to wave goodbye, he felt confident, now that he'd met Claire Lamontagne, that he wouldn't need an alarm on his phone to remind him to think about her.

Claire might have thought her trip into town had been a complete waste of time if not for the fact that she had dinner plans with her best friend. But it wasn't Sarah who was on her mind as she sipped her iced tea and pretended to peruse Diggers' menu—it was Sarah's unexpectedly hunky cousin.

She'd been certain she knew what to expect when she pressed the doorbell. According to Sarah, her cousin was *seriously introverted and more than a little socially awkward.* But she'd promised her friend that when it came to computers, there was no one who knew more than Devin.

So Claire had been prepared to meet a tech geek, and maybe Devin Blake was that. But he was also ridiculously attractive, and she hadn't been prepared for the gut-punch of awareness that hit her when he opened the door.

It had been a long time since she'd experienced such an immediate and intense response to a man—

and while it should have been a relief to know that her broken heart had mended, she would have been happier still if she hadn't responded to her best friend's cousin. Because the absolute last thing she needed right now was the complication of an attraction that she had no intention of ever acting on.

"You're frowning," Sarah noted, as she slid into the vacant booth across from Claire. "Why are you frowning?"

She consciously smoothed her brow and offered her friend a smile. "Hello to you, too."

"What's wrong?" Sarah pressed. "Did the meeting with Devin not go well?"

"Actually, the meeting didn't go at all."

Her friend sighed. "He completely forgot about it, didn't he?"

"That's the impression I got."

"Probably because I didn't specifically remind him to put the date and time in his calendar."

"Is he that much of a scatterbrain?" Claire asked, starting to rethink the whole plan. Not that she didn't appreciate Sarah's recommendation—and the possibility that Devin might be willing to do the work at a discounted rate—but she really wanted to get her website up sooner rather than later.

"He's that much of a genius," Sarah clarified. "Sometimes, when his attention is focused on something else, he doesn't pay enough attention to a conversation to retain the details afterward."

Before Claire could respond, their server stopped by to take their order.

Though Sarah hadn't even opened her menu, both women had eaten at the local bar and grill often enough over the years that they had the contents memorized.

"I'll have the buttermilk fried chicken with mashed potatoes and gravy," Claire said.

"Spinach salad with grilled chicken and soda water with a twist of lime," Sarah added.

"That sounds a lot healthier than what I'm having," Claire acknowledged.

The server turned back, notepad still in hand. "Did you want to change your order?"

"No way." But Claire softened her response with a smile. "And make sure the cook doesn't skimp on the gravy."

Sarah sighed. "If I ate like you, I'd need a whole new wardrobe within a week."

"Come out to Twilight Valley and help me muck out stalls every day and you won't have to worry about calorie counts."

"Thanks, but I like my desk job. Well, most of the time."

"Rough day?" Claire asked.

"Not rough, but not particularly interesting, either. So let's talk about yours instead—and why you were frowning when I came in."

"I was just wondering if maybe I should find someone else to build my website," she said.

Her friend winced. "Did Devin really make such a bad impression?"

"No," she admitted.

In fact, he hadn't made a bad impression at all.

Even now, remembering the intensity in his hazel eyes flecked with gold, Claire felt a stirring of something low in her belly that she didn't want to acknowledge.

No more men. No more heartbreak.

For the past seven months, that had been her mantra—a promise to herself. And not once, in all that time, had she been tempted to break that promise. But now, after one brief meeting with Devin Blake, her hormones were clamoring, urging her to reconsider.

Not going to happen.

"Did he indicate that he didn't want to do it?"

The question snapped Claire out of her reverie and back to the present. "What?"

"Did Devin say that he didn't want to set up your website?"

"No," she said again.

"Then give him another chance," Sarah urged.

"I will." But only because she needed a website. "If he actually shows up at Twilight Valley on Thursday."

"Inviting him to the ranch was a great idea," her friend enthused. "He'll be able to see firsthand what you're doing and why the website is so important."

"That was only part of my rationale. The bigger part was that, if he forgets about our meeting again, at least I won't have wasted time trekking into town."

"Is it really a waste when it gives you an excuse to have dinner with your BFF?" Sarah asked, feigning hurt.

"You know I'm happy to come into town to see you anytime," Claire said, smiling her thanks to the server as he delivered their plates to the table. "But I'm even happier in blue jeans and cowboy boots."

"I don't know why you felt you had to dress up to meet with Devin, but it's nice to see you wearing something other than blue jeans and cowboy boots for a change."

Sarah's comment reminded Claire that she had a whole closet full of fancy clothes that she had no use for anymore. She'd had fun shopping for and wearing them when she lived in Texas, but they were wholly unsuitable for her new life in Nevada, and she made a mental note to box them up and drop them off at the women's shelter in Battle Mountain at her earliest opportunity.

"Cowboy boots are comfortable," she said now, dipping her fork into the mound of potatoes smothered in gravy. "These shoes—not so much. I don't know how you manage to walk around in heels all day—every day—and not break an ankle."

"Practice," Sarah said simply, poking at her salad.

"If I practiced wearing heels in the barn, I'd definitely break an ankle."

"You're right," her friend agreed, a sudden sparkle in her eyes. "Luckily, I know a better place for you to practice."

Claire didn't ask.

Sarah answered anyway. "Las Vegas."

"Or I could stick to wearing cowboy boots," she suggested—a much more preferable alternative, in her opinion.

"I'm serious," Sarah said.

"So am I."

Her friend chewed on a mouthful of leafy greens. "You've been working too hard lately—you deserve a break. And it's been a long time since we've had a girls' weekend."

"I don't know about a weekend, but I could use a spa day," Claire admitted. Because a break sounded good, but time with her BFF sounded even better.

"A weekend in Vegas," Sarah insisted, opening a search engine on her phone to browse options. "With a spa suite at Aria. Or maybe we should book at The Palazzo, to take advantage of everything Canyon Ranch has to offer. Or Caesars Palace. Have you experienced the Arctic Ice room?"

Claire shook her head.

"You'll love it," her friend promised, as she continued to scroll through hotel options. "Let's book something for the end of the month."

"It all sounds fabulous." Tempting—and very pricey. "But there's no way I could leave the ranch for a whole weekend."

Sarah pouted. "There's no point in going to Vegas for a day."

"So we'll indulge ourselves with a few hours at Serenity," she said, referring to the local spa.

"We can do that another time. I really want to go to Vegas the last weekend of May."

Claire sliced off a piece of chicken and popped it into her mouth. "What's happening in Vegas the last weekend of May that you so desperately want to be there?" she asked, after she'd finished chewing.

Sarah looked at her with concern. "It's not what's happening there but what's *not* happening here."

"Huh?"

"Do you honestly expect me to believe that you forgot?"

Frowning, she opened the calendar app on her phone and skipped to the end of May. "Oh."

"You really did," Sarah realized, stunned.

Claire nodded slowly, feeling a little stunned herself. "I forgot my wedding day."

Chapter Two

Seven months earlier, when Claire had taken the two-carat diamond off her finger, she'd been heartbroken to accept that the life she'd dreamed of with Eric Perry wasn't ever going to be a reality. Ending their engagement had been the right thing to do—she'd had no doubts about that even if she'd had nothing but doubts about her future.

She hadn't planned to come back to Haven. In fact, she'd been sitting in her car in the parking lot of the apartment that she'd shared with her fiancé, the back seat packed with everything she owned, staring at the map on her phone and trying to decide where to go next, when Sarah called. She'd been grateful for her friend's invitation to stay with her while she figured out her next move. Then, shortly after her return, she'd learned that

Aunt Susan and Uncle Mick were selling their ranch and moving to California to be closer to their daughters.

Claire had been as devastated by that news as she'd been by her recent breakup, because in the few weeks that she'd been home, she'd discovered how much she'd missed her friends and family—and especially the ranch. But now the house that had been her childhood refuge was her home and a small part of what had been the Cartwright Ranch was Twilight Valley—a haven for horses.

Across the table, Sarah was looking at her with concern. "So…you're really okay?"

"I'm really okay," Claire said.

And it was true.

In fact, she was better than okay, because she finally had a sense of direction and a feeling of purpose at Twilight Valley.

"I'm glad," Sarah said. "Although I'm still disappointed that you don't want to go to Vegas."

"I'll make it up to you," Claire promised.

"How are you going to do that?"

She grinned. "By sharing my cheesecake."

Her friend groaned. "You really are the devil."

But she didn't protest when Claire ordered, asking for extra whipped cream and two forks, and she couldn't seem to tear her gaze away from the plate after the dessert was delivered.

"You know where you can get a fabulous cheesecake?" Sarah asked, before immediately answering her own question. "The Bellagio Patisserie in Las Vegas."

"This cheesecake right here is pretty fabulous, too,"

Claire said, nudging the plate closer to her friend's side of the table.

Sarah finally picked up the second fork. "Okay, this is good," she acknowledged, her mouth full of rich and creamy deliciousness.

Claire scooped up some more cake—with extra whipped cream. "I've been thinking about something."

"Shh." Her friend's eyes were closed. "This is the closest I've been to an orgasm in… I don't know how long."

Claire laughed, then immediately sobered. "I bet my dry spell has been longer."

Sarah opened her eyes. "It's not a contest—or, if it is, it's not one that either one of us should want to win."

"Maybe we should order another piece of cake."

Her friend shook her head regretfully. "Maybe you should tell me what you were going to say when you interrupted my foodgasm."

"I've had a lot of time to think…since Eric and I broke up."

"It's natural to want to know what went wrong in a relationship," Sarah noted. "But with respect to your relationship, *he's* what went wrong."

"Or maybe I was as much to blame as he was for things not working out," she mused.

Her friend arched a brow. "Did you suddenly change who you were and your expectations of the relationship?"

"No," Claire said.

"Then how are you to blame?"

"Because I'm not sure I really loved him."

Sarah took a moment to ponder that confession— or maybe she was just savoring the last bite of cheesecake—before she asked, "Then why did you say yes to his proposal?"

"Believe me, I've asked myself that exact question more times than I can count."

"And have you come up with an answer?" her friend prompted.

"Not one that I'm particularly proud of," Claire confided. "I think I said yes because marrying Eric would have given me a reason to stay in Texas."

"You had a job and an apartment in Texas before you ever met him," Sarah pointed out.

She nodded. "But everything still felt temporary to me—as if I was just delaying my return home. Even at Perry Brothers Construction, I started out as a temp."

"And then, after only six months, you were offered a full-time job."

Which meant that she'd finally been able to move out of a shared studio apartment and into a one-bedroom of her own. Two years after that, she'd moved in with Eric—and been left without a home when she'd given him back his ring and his key.

"And still, every time I spoke to my parents—" which was every Sunday night "—they asked when I was going to come home. As if it was a given that I would return to Haven, regardless of how many times I told them that I was happy living in Austin."

"And then Eric proposed."

She nodded. "And finally my mom accepted that I was making a life somewhere else—was even happy about it—because I was going to have a husband to take care of me."

"As if you couldn't take care of yourself," Sarah said indignantly.

Claire shrugged. "You know my mom."

Elsa Wallingford had been a high school teacher of world history and social studies who'd routinely attended protests to draw attention to inequalities and injustices around the globe before she'd met and fallen in love with Paul Lamontagne.

After they married and she got pregnant, her priorities had shifted, and she'd given up teaching to be a stay-at-home wife and mother who deferred to her preacher husband about almost everything.

It had been Elsa's choice—of that Claire had no doubt. She just wished she'd been afforded the same opportunity to make her own choices, without constantly being reminded of mistakes that she'd made in the past.

"I do know your mom," Sarah agreed. "Which is why I understood your eagerness to go away to college— and your reluctance to come home after graduation."

"I was more than reluctant. I was certain I never wanted to come back, but it wasn't nearly as difficult as I thought it would be," she confided. "I mean, it was hard to admit that I'd fallen in love with the wrong man—*again*—but when I drove past the Welcome to Haven sign on the highway, it suddenly struck me how much I'd missed being here."

"How much you missed your best friend, you mean," Sarah said.

Claire smiled. "I did miss you most of all."

"Okay, then," her friend said, placated by the response.

"I didn't miss my parents nearly as much as I should have." She felt only a little bit guilty for confessing that truth, because it was the truth and because she knew she could trust her best friend to take her secrets to the grave. "And I definitely didn't miss feeling as if every move I made was being judged—and found wanting."

"Your parents are the polar opposite of mine," Sarah acknowledged. "Derrick and Lizbeth never really cared what their kids were doing."

It wasn't much of an exaggeration. Claire had spent a fair amount of time with her friend while they were growing up, because at Sarah's house they were free to hang out and watch TV without anyone reminding them that homework needed to come first—or shutting off the television even after their studying was done because the program they'd chosen was inappropriate. At Sarah's house, they weren't offered homemade cookies or oven-baked potato chips but could help themselves to whatever (and as much as) they wanted from a pantry stocked with goodies made by Little Debbie and Frito-Lay.

"At least so long as we didn't end up in the hospital. Or in jail," Sarah continued.

"And even when you ended up in jail, they bailed you out."

"That only happened *once*. And how was I supposed to know that Zack didn't have permission to borrow the car he was driving?"

"Because it was an Audi and he was a seventeen-year-old being raised by a single mom who drove a school bus."

"Okay, maybe I should have asked some questions," Sarah allowed.

But Claire had always suspected that her friend had wanted to get in trouble, to force her parents to pay attention. And it had worked—at least in the moment.

Sarah had been lucky to be released with a slap on the wrist, but Zack—who couldn't claim it was his first run-in with the law or that he had the owner's okay to take the car from the auto shop where he worked part-time after school—had done six months in juvie.

"Do you ever hear from Zack anymore?" Claire asked her friend now.

"We exchange messages on Facebook every now and again. In fact, he sent me a picture of his new car a few months back—an Audi Q5."

Claire chuckled. "Obviously he's doing okay for himself."

"He's a lawyer, if you can believe it."

"Actually, I can," she realized. "He was always smart. Angry and defiant, but also smart."

"And sexy," Sarah added, with just a hint of wistfulness in her tone.

Obviously Claire and her friend had different definitions of "sexy," because while Sarah was reminiscing about her dark and broody lover from long ago, Claire was thinking about a much more recent acquaintance—and already counting the hours until she would see Devin Blake again.

It continued to be a source of frustration to Devin that the senior executives at Blake Mining refused to consider virtual meetings. As the supervisor of IT, he could easily have set it up so that the department heads could give their reports from almost anywhere. His uncle Derrick—Sarah's dad—had seemed intrigued by the idea when Devin proposed it, but his own mom had immediately shut down all discussion of the possibility.

Lorraine Blake was adamant that everyone needed to show up and take their places around the big table in the boardroom as they'd always done. Devin suspected his mother's stubborn insistence wasn't about tradition so much as control, because everyone spent more time drinking coffee and planning family events than discussing actual business. Or maybe she insisted on these monthly meetings to ensure her youngest son left his house at least once a month.

It was true that when he was immersed in a project, Devin sometimes lost track of time. And, once or twice, even the day of the week. No doubt that was why Tamara Benson managed the IT department, handling the day-to-day issues onsite while Devin mostly worked from home, troubleshooting bigger problems.

He had an office at Blake Mining, of course, but he preferred to be in his own space, where distractions were limited. He wasn't antisocial, exactly, though he knew there were others who described him that way. The truth was, he had a small group of close friends with whom he could talk for hours about almost anything. He just wasn't comfortable making conversation with people he didn't know.

And sometimes his tongue got a little tangled around attractive women.

Since Claire Lamontagne was essentially a stranger—and also incredibly hot—he suspected it would take a concerted effort on his part to get through their rescheduled meeting without affirming her suspicion that he was the complete idiot he'd appeared to be when she showed up at his door.

He glanced at his watch.

9:25.

Thankfully, he had some time to get his head into the right space before seeing her again.

"Want to grab a coffee at Sweet Caroline's?" Trevor asked, falling into step beside his brother as they exited the conference room after the meeting had concluded.

Devin glanced at his watch again.

9:26.

"Sure," he agreed. "I've got about an hour to kill."

Though Trevor's brows lifted, he didn't comment on his brother's reply.

When they were seated inside the bakery and café with their drinks—and a fresh-out-of-the-oven cinnamon roll for Trevor, who hadn't had time for breakfast after his toddler son threw up on him, necessitating a complete change of clothes for both.

"Is Aidan okay?" Devin asked, immediately concerned about his nephew.

"He'll be fine—but my tie's in the trash."

"I didn't ask about your tie."

"Haylee's not worried," Trevor assured him. "She suspects they picked up some kind of bug at story time on Tuesday, because Ellie was sick yesterday."

"So why, instead of rushing home to help your wife

take care of your sick twins, are you here drinking coffee with me?"

"Because I need your help."

"Caring for sick kids isn't really my area of expertise," he pointed out.

"It wasn't mine, either," his brother confided. "Believe me, parenthood has a way of teaching you some hard lessons—and fast."

"I'll take your word for it," he said.

Not that he didn't want to be a father—maybe— someday. But it wasn't anything he'd given much thought to because that day, if it ever came, was far in the future.

"But that's not why I need your help," Trevor continued.

Devin dumped two packets of sugar into his cup, stirred. "So tell me what you need."

"I'm planning something special for Haylee, for our anniversary."

He frowned. "Your anniversary isn't until December."

"We got married in December," Trevor agreed.

"You have another anniversary?"

His brother feigned interest in his cinnamon bun, a smile tugging at the corners of his mouth. "We're coming up on the second anniversary of the night we met."

At Brielle and Caleb's wedding, Devin remembered, because he'd been there, too. And he'd witnessed firsthand how entranced his brother had been with the woman in the pink dress. So much so that Trevor had followed her all the way to California to ask for a second date.

"How can I help?" he asked.

"Well, you're one of very few people that Haylee trusts with the twins. Obviously her sister is another, but Finley lives in California. Brielle and Caleb are also on the short list, but obviously I'm not going to ask them to watch Aidan and Ellie on their anniversary."

"You want me to babysit," Devin realized.

His brother nodded.

"Sure," he readily agreed.

Trevor grinned. "Great, because I've already booked the Annie Oakley Room at The Stagecoach Inn."

"I'd never claim to be an expert when it comes to romance—" in fact, *neophyte* would be a much more accurate term "—but wouldn't spending the night in the Wild Bill Getaway Suite be more special?"

"The penthouse is bigger and fancier," Trevor noted. "But the first night Haylee and I spent together was in the Annie Oakley Room."

The night their twins were conceived.

Not that Trevor had ever said as much, but considering that the wedding was in June and Aidan and Ellie were born in March, Devin would have managed to put the pieces together even if he hadn't been a genius.

"I never knew you had such a sentimental streak."

His brother shrugged. "I'm madly in love with my wife and don't care who knows it."

"Trust me—*everyone* knows it," Devin assured him. "Now tell me what's going on with you."

"What do you mean?"

"You said you had an hour to kill," Trevor noted. "An

hour until what? Do you have a hot date at eleven a.m. on a Thursday morning?"

"A business meeting," Devin clarified.

"Business?" his brother echoed, sounding surprised. "Anything I should know about?"

He shook his head. "It's not Blake Mining business."

Trevor broke off a piece of cinnamon roll with his fork. "Let me guess." But first he popped the warm pastry into his mouth, chewed and swallowed. "You developed another app you're selling?"

"No. Well, yes," Devin admitted. "But that's not what the meeting is about, either." He sipped his coffee. "Apparently I'm going to be designing a website."

"You hate designing websites," Trevor remarked, sounding amused.

"And yet, people still ask me to do it," he noted ruefully.

"Which one of our relatives hit you up this time?" his brother asked, understanding that "people" usually meant family.

"Our cousin Sarah."

"Why does the Associate Director of Occupational Safety and Health at Blake Mining need a website?"

"It's not actually for her, but for a friend of hers."

"A female friend?" his brother guessed.

"Yeah. The one with the horse rescue." Devin pulled his phone out of his pocket and glanced at the meeting notation, as if he needed to look up the details to be reminded of her name. As if it—and her image—hadn't been indelibly stamped on his memory at their first meeting. "Claire Lamontagne."

"So…is she hot?"

Devin scowled at the question. "You're married—and madly in love with your wife," he said, echoing his brother's own words. "Not to mention a father. Of twins."

Trevor grinned. "So you *do* think she's hot."

"She's a friend of Sarah's," he said again.

"Uh-huh." His brother smirked. "Now I know why you shaved today."

"I shaved because, when I show up at the office without shaving, Mom worries that I'm not taking care of myself."

Or, if she didn't actually worry, she nevertheless remarked on his unprofessional appearance.

As if there was ever anyone but family at the meetings.

"And the tie?" Trevor prompted.

"Okay, so maybe I didn't make a great impression when I first met Claire," Devin confided. "I'm hoping she'll forget about that today."

"With a tie covered in—" his brother leaned forward for a closer look "—I don't even know what that is."

"HTML code," Devin said.

"Because you want to be sure she knows that you're a total computer nerd?" Trevor guessed.

"Because I like this tie that—in case you don't remember—you and your wife gave me for Christmas."

"I remember," his brother said, though not very convincingly. "So what happened that you didn't make a good first impression? Or maybe I can guess—you forgot about the meeting, didn't you?"

"I'm not sure Sarah actually specified a date and time," he felt compelled to point out in his defense.

Trevor chuckled. "Well, I don't want to be responsible for you being late to *this* meeting, so I won't hold you up any longer. Just…be careful."

Devin swallowed the last mouthful of his coffee. "Why do you think I need to be careful?"

"Because if Sarah put this woman in your path, it might be a setup."

"You can't mean a romantic setup."

"You don't think she'd try to play matchmaker for her friend—and her cousin?" his brother challenged.

He immediately shook his head. "I'm hardly Claire's type."

Trevor frowned. "If you only just met this woman, how could you possibly know her type?"

"I guess I don't," he acknowledged. "It's just that she seemed so friendly and personable and…"

Stunningly beautiful, though Devin was smart enough not to say that part out loud.

"And you're so unfriendly and disagreeable?"

Of course, his brother could joke about such things, because Trevor had always had a way with women. Devin, not so much. Or rather, not at all.

He'd gone out on the occasional date, usually to prove to his family that he wasn't antisocial, but he'd always been more comfortable at home, with his own company.

His buddy Gavin had urged him to check out Tinder, claiming that it was a great way to meet women who wanted to get laid. Devin had thanked him for the advice and made a mental note to stay far away from the app. Casual sex wasn't really his scene, for a lot of reasons, none of which he felt inclined to share with Gavin. And none of which he was going to share with Trevor, either.

Instead, he carried his empty cup to the counter, waved goodbye to his brother and walked out the door.

Chapter Three

Claire wasn't consciously watching the clock, but as she finished grooming Crescent Moon—named for the distinctively shaped irregular star on her face—she kept stealing glances at the time display on her Fitbit. She'd kept busy with her usual chores earlier that morning and then, because she'd been hot and sweaty, gone back to the house to take a shower.

Of course, she'd be even hotter and sweatier before the day was through, but she didn't want to face Devin looking like a ranch hand, even if that was exactly what she was. So she'd scrubbed away the dirt and grime, moisturized her skin with her favorite lotion, and dressed again in a clean pair of jeans and a pink T-shirt with white flowers embroidered around the V-neck.

"Why do I even care what he thinks of me?" she

asked the old mare, who was patiently submitting to her ministrations. "Is it because he's my best friend's cousin? Or because I felt something…unexpected… when he opened the door Monday afternoon?" Something she'd been certain she didn't ever want to feel again when she came back from Texas.

"Maybe I was just caught off guard. Because Sarah said he was a genius, but he's also a total hottie." Her strokes were gentle as she moved the soft brush over the horse's cheek. "Somehow, knowing that he's as smart as he is good-looking only makes him hotter.

"But I only want help with my website," she continued. "I'm not looking to get romantically involved. I've been down that road too many times already and it always leads to the same destination—heartbreak."

And still, there was no denying that her female parts had taken notice of the fact that Devin Blake was pure male.

Or maybe she'd only imagined the flutter low in her belly.

She sighed then and shook her head. "And I'm having a heart-to-heart with a horse, because you're the only one I can talk to about the fact that my heart is racing just thinking about the fact that he might come out here today, even if I'm not entirely convinced he's going to show. It's quite possible that he'll forget this meeting just like he forgot the last one."

She switched the soft brush for a wide-tooth comb and shifted her attention to Crescent Moon's mane. "I feel ridiculous. Like I'm in high school again, with butterflies in my stomach whenever I walked past Jacob Nolan's locker on my way to the cafeteria.

"Of course, Jacob Nolan turned out to be a total jerk, so maybe that's not a good comparison. Or maybe it is," she decided. "Maybe that memory should be a reminder of my abysmal taste in men and that, if I like Devin Blake, then he's probably going to turn out to be a jerk, too."

"Or maybe he won't."

Claire spun around to see the man himself standing inside the open door of the barn.

Her gaze dropped to her Fitbit as heat rose to her face.

10:48

Dammit, he was *early*.

And her cheeks were burning with humiliation.

"I need to get a dog," she muttered under her breath.

"A warning system?" Devin guessed, smiling just a little.

"You're early," she pointed out.

"If I remember correctly, you told me to come whenever I was finished up at Blake Mining."

"If you're as smart as Sarah says, I have no doubt you always remember correctly," she retorted. "Except when it comes to remembering dates and times of meetings that aren't important to you."

He didn't actually blush, but she noticed a hint of color creeping up his neck. And maybe she should have felt a measure of satisfaction that she'd managed to turn the tables on him, because she'd been embarrassed that he'd caught her talking about him—to a horse! Instead she felt guilty, because he hadn't really done anything wrong and she was being unkind.

"I remembered this one," he said.

She nodded. "So I see."

She saw, too, that he was wearing jeans again, but instead of a faded Pearl Jam concert T-shirt, today he'd donned an actual shirt and tie—a lilac button-down with a darker purple tie covered with what looked like random letters and numbers. Of course, it was Nevada, so she wasn't at all surprised to see the cowboy boots on his feet.

The outfit shouldn't have worked, and yet, looking at him now, she felt that flutter again. *Dammit.*

"I didn't realize that Twilight Valley was the new name of Cartwright Ranch," he said.

She appreciated his effort to make small talk, to smooth over the sudden awkwardness between them.

"Actually, Twilight Valley is only a small part of the original ranch," she told him.

She clipped a lead onto Crescent Moon's bridle and guided the horse outside to the paddock.

As Devin fell into step beside her, Claire continued her explanation. "Most of it was sold to David Gilmore, adding to the acreage of the Circle G."

"As if he doesn't already own more land than anyone else in the whole county," he remarked.

It was a true enough statement—only the slight edge in his tone reminded her that there was bad blood between the Blakes and the Gilmores going back several generations. She wasn't entirely clear on all the details of the age-old feud, though she knew it had started with a land dispute and was later exacerbated by a tragic romance.

In any event, the marriage of Brielle Channing, whose mom was a Blake, to Caleb Gilmore—and the birth of their son—had finally bridged the gap between the two families.

"You've got goats," Devin noted, pausing at the fence as Claire opened the gate for the horse.

She smiled as she glanced over at the stout-bodied animals frolicking in the grass. "Lily and Daisy."

"I thought this was an equine facility."

"It is," she confirmed. "The goats are companions for the horses."

"Because horses are herd animals," he noted.

"And some of them, when they first arrive, might not be ready to be introduced to the herd."

"You're referring to animals that have been abused or neglected," he realized.

She nodded. "Your grandfather raises and trains horses, doesn't he?"

"He used to—now it's my cousin Spencer who does the same. But despite his age and arthritis, Gramps still helps out as much as he can."

He followed her again when she returned to the barn.

"Who's this?" he asked.

She turned to see that Devin had paused at the stall that housed the ranch's newest resident. "That's Midnight."

"Hey, there," he crooned, lifting a hand to reach over the gate.

"He doesn't like…"

Claire's words trailed off when the animal held perfectly still and allowed Devin to rub its cheek, then run a hand down his long neck. His touch was steady and sure, and after a moment, Midnight closed his eyes, apparently completely at ease with this stranger's touch.

She watched in disbelief as he continued to stroke the animal, and found herself fantasizing about the kind of magic he might be able to work on a woman with those hands—and wishing she might find out.

"You were saying?"

"What?" She felt her cheeks flush as she wondered if he'd caught her—once again—speaking her thoughts aloud.

"He doesn't like…" Devin prompted.

"Strangers," Claire finished. "And usually he doesn't, but he seems okay with you."

He shrugged. "I like animals and they like me."

"I can see that," she acknowledged, as she reassessed his attire along with her planned approach for their meeting. "Do you ride?"

He looked insulted by the question. "Of course I ride."

"Good," she said.

And with that, Claire Lamontagne pivoted on her heel, leaving Devin frowning at her back.

Of course, the frown didn't remain on his face for long, his confusion shifting to admiration as he watched her hips sway as she walked away.

He hadn't been able to forget how she'd looked when she'd shown up at his house Monday afternoon, and every time he thought about her—and he'd thought about her *a lot*—he'd been certain he'd never met anyone half as beautiful. She was dressed more casually today, but she was equally stunning in a simple T-shirt and snug-fitting denim with her hair braided—and still so far out of his league he couldn't even see the ballpark.

Except that she'd called him a hottie.

Somehow, knowing that he's as smart as he is good-looking only makes him hotter.

Even with her words echoing in his head, he was still stunned by the possibility that she could be attracted to him.

Of course, his clumsy announcement of his presence and her discovery that he'd overheard her confession might have killed any vestige of attraction she'd been feeling in that moment. Because awkward interactions with women were the story of his life.

She glanced over her shoulder and caught him staring.

A perfectly arched brow lifted. "Are you coming?"

He had no idea where she was leading him, but he knew it didn't matter—he would follow wherever she wanted to go.

It turned out she was only leading him as far as the tack room, so that he could pick a saddle.

"I've got a couple of volunteers who help out with the horses, but they don't always get as much exercise as they should," she explained, as they worked side by side, tacking the mounts she'd chosen.

"Ready?" she asked.

He nodded, and reached up for the saddle horn, prepared to mount the bay stallion she'd assigned to him.

"Wait." She looped the reins in her hand around a fence post, then breached the distance between them and lifted her hand to his tie. "You're a little overdressed for where we're going."

He swallowed as her fingers—long and slender, with neatly trimmed and unpainted nails—loosened the knot at his throat. Then she tugged on one end, pulling the tie free from his collar before moving on to release the top button.

Her movements were brisk and impersonal, and at the same time, there was something incredibly intimate about her actions. She paused then, as if suddenly realizing the same thing. Her fingertips rested lightly on the placket of his shirt as she lifted her eyes to his.

The air between them crackled with electricity.

She stood there for a long moment, their gazes locked together. His heart hammered against his ribs; desire rushed through his veins. But he held himself perfectly still, waiting for her next move.

Her hand dropped away from his chest and she took a careful step back, moving her lips into a smile.

"That's better," she said, draping his tie over the rail. "Now you look relaxed and ready to ride."

Maybe it was true, but he sure as hell didn't feel relaxed. Instead, every one of his nerve endings was as taut as the string on Zelda's Bow of Light.

As he watched Claire effortlessly mount her horse, he silently cursed his cousin for setting her friend in his path—because that relationship was only one of too many reasons why he knew he shouldn't act on the feelings that burned in his gut.

Claire wasn't surprised to learn that Devin could ride, but she hadn't expected that he would look so completely at ease on horseback—as if he was born a cowboy. Watching him move over the fields on the back of Hades, her heart fluttered again. She'd spent a lot of time at her uncle's ranch when she was younger, so she'd seen plenty of men on horseback, but none of them had ever made her mouth go dry just from looking at them.

She was no stranger to attraction. Since the first rush of hormones had hit her system at the onset of puberty, she'd experienced countless crushes and imagined herself in love more than a few times. Maybe it had even been the real deal once or twice, but she couldn't remember feeling quite like this.

No more men. No more heartbreak.

Even as she repeated the mantra inside her head, she wanted to believe that Devin was different.

And wasn't that her problem?

Whenever she felt that fluttery feeling in her belly, she was certain that this time would be different.

And every time, it had been exactly the same.

Every time, she ended up alone.

She pressed her heels into Oswald's side, urging him to go faster, as if doing so might allow Claire to outrun the niggling thoughts in her mind.

But she couldn't outrun Devin and Hades, who kept stride with them all the way to the creek. She dismounted, then led Oswald to the water. Devin did the same with Hades.

As the horses drank their fill, Claire looked around, a smile curving her lips.

"Even after almost six months, it still gives me a thrill to know that this land—the one place where I always felt I belonged—is actually mine," she confided to Devin.

"You spent a lot of time here while you were growing up?"

"As much as Uncle Mick and Aunt Susan would let me—and my cousins Joss and Dee would tolerate me."

"You're an only child?" he guessed.

She shook her head. "No, I'm the youngest of three—and only girl—so I was often left behind by my older brothers. Of course, Joseph and Thomas were encouraged to include me in their games and activities, but I didn't want to hang out with them any more than they wanted me hanging out with them.

"And then came the magical summer of my cousin Dee's tenth birthday."

"What was so magical about it?" he asked curiously.

"After the cake was eaten and presents opened, Joss—older than me and Dee by two years—left to go to a friend's house for a sleepover, and Dee pouted that she should get to have a sleepover, too, so Aunt Susan invited me to spend the night at the ranch."

"And that was a big deal?"

"A very big deal," Claire confirmed. "My parents had never let me go to a sleepover before that."

And she'd held her breath, waiting for her mother or

father to trample the blossoming hope inside her. For it to be pointed out that she had a perfectly good bed in her own home and didn't need to sleep in someone else's, which was the response they'd given whenever she'd been invited to her friend Sarah's house in the past.

But for whatever reason, they'd decided that spending the night at her aunt and uncle's home was more acceptable than staying with a friend and agreed to Susan's request.

"We didn't stay up particularly late and we didn't get stomachaches from eating too much junk food—although we did get another slice of cake with ice cream before we had to brush our teeth for bed. But we did all the things that I always wanted to do—like grooming the horses and feeding the chickens."

"So you always wanted to do chores?" He didn't sound impressed.

"They didn't feel like chores," she said, though she could see why he might think so. "But that wasn't all we did. We also took turns on the tire swing and skipped rocks on the pond."

"And that was your idea of fun?"

"I was ten," she reminded him. "And I'd led a very sheltered life until then."

She didn't tell him that, after she and Dee were in their pj's, they got to watch a movie—*The Princess Diaries*—that Claire knew her mom would never let her watch at home. Not because it was inappropriate in any way, but because it didn't serve a purpose. In the Lamontagne house, television was usually restricted to educational programming, with only rare exceptions made.

After the movie, the girls were tucked into sleeping bags on the floor of Dee's room, because according to Joss it wasn't really a sleepover unless you slept on the floor. Claire had tossed and turned for a long time, because the floor was hard and uncomfortable. And still, it was at that point—and for a long time after—the best night of her life.

When she'd left Haven to go to college, she'd been almost desperate to escape. She'd wanted—*needed*—to live her own life, free of her parents' restrictions and unencumbered by their expectations. She'd been so eager to get away from everything she was certain she hated about the small town that she'd let herself forget all the things she loved.

Or maybe she'd needed to forget—to wipe the slate clean so that she could start over. And Texas had been fun for a while. Eight years in fact. But the Lone Star State had never really felt like home, not even after the better part of a decade. Not even when she'd been planning a life in Austin with Eric.

She'd made a narrow escape there—and not an easy one.

But she wasn't going to ruin this beautiful day by thinking about her former fiancé now. Today she was going to focus on only good stuff.

She had so many happy memories of times spent here on the ranch, and she was determined to make a lot more going forward. Not just for herself, but for

Toby, Hades, Oswald, Midnight, Regina, Bolt and all the other horses yet to come.

"So what inspired you to buy your aunt and uncle's ranch?" Devin asked.

"Finding out that they planned to sell it."

She shouldn't have been surprised by their decision. Josslyn, who'd always wanted to be a doctor, was now an internist in San Diego; Deanna, who'd dreamed of being a lawyer—to sue incompetent doctors, she used to tease her sister—had a successful litigation practice in Los Angeles. And Mick and Susan wanted, understandably, to be closer to their daughters.

"Well, your parents must have been happy when you moved home," he said.

"I think they're happy that I'm back in Haven, but they don't really approve of what I'm doing here at Twilight Valley. Or maybe it would be more accurate to say that they worry about me," she allowed. "Because I'm a young woman living alone in the country, and because working with horses, even well-trained horses, can be dangerous."

"And I'd guess that many of the horses that find their way here haven't received much training at all."

"And you'd be right," she confirmed. "Which is all the more reason that what I'm doing matters. But when I refused to be dissuaded by their arguments, my mom and dad sicced my brothers on me."

And what did it say about her relationship with them that the first time they reached out after her return to Haven was at the behest of their parents? At the very least, it said that Joseph and Thomas were more concerned about honoring their mother and father than they were about their sister or what she wanted.

"Obviously they weren't any more successful," Devin noted.

"No," she agreed.

But she'd been happy to see Thomas when he stopped by. He was married with four kids—teenagers now—and busy, so she appreciated that he'd taken the time to visit even if he couldn't be supportive. Joseph had called a few days later. He and his wife and their four kids lived in Reno, so it wasn't as convenient for him to drop in, but they had a nice chat.

Still, the truth was, she really didn't know either of her brothers anymore, and she wasn't sure she'd recognize any of her nieces and nephews if she passed them on the sidewalk. It was partly her fault, she knew, because she'd chosen to move away. But even when she'd returned to Nevada, she was rarely invited to visit, and she suspected that was because her brothers worried that she'd be a bad influence on their daughters.

Claire had always been the black sheep of the family—the one who tested boundaries and flaunted conventions without ever really understanding why. Growing up, she *wanted* to be good, she just didn't have it in her to be quiet and obedient. And she didn't think it was fair that her brothers were given so much freedom to do what they wanted while she was always being reminded of the rules.

Which, of course, only made her more determined to break those rules.

But now *she* was the one making the rules—and she needed to remember that one of those rules was to ignore the fluttery sensation in her belly whenever she was around Devin Blake.

Chapter Four

"Well, I'm glad you suggested this," Devin said. "It's a beautiful day for a ride—and a long time since I've taken time out to enjoy something like this."

"I'll bet you wouldn't guess that only three months ago Hades wouldn't let a rider on his back," Claire told him.

"You'd be right," he confirmed.

"He had a lot of different owners—and a lot of inconsistent training—in his nine years, leaving him confused and afraid."

"He doesn't seem confused or afraid now."

"He's come a long way," she agreed. "In a few more months, he might even be ready for a new home, if I can find the right placement for him."

"You don't want to keep him here?"

"It's not about want—it's about space," she explained. "As much as I might like to, I can't keep them all. But I also won't let any of them go until I've found what I believe is the best possible home for them."

"So why a horse rescue?" he asked, then immediately corrected himself. "I mean, why an equine rehabilitation and retirement facility?"

"I fell in love with horses when I was young," she confided. "But it wasn't until I was working and living in Austin that I realized there are countless injured, abused and neglected animals that end up at auctions and kill pens."

"How did you come to that realization in the big city?"

"My boss had more money than you could imagine…" She sent Devin a sideways glance. "Well, you're a Blake, so I'm sure *you* could imagine. Anyway, one of his hobbies was horses. Breeding and training, primarily, but he also had an interest in saving horses from slaughter. He had a whole crew of trainers and volunteers who worked with rescued horses to rehabilitate and rehome them, and eventually I became one of those volunteers.

"It was somehow both heartbreaking and rewarding," she confided now. "And when I decided to leave Austin, the hardest part was leaving Storm's Shelter—named for the first horse Arthur Perry rescued."

"Why did you leave Austin?" he asked her now.

She waved a hand dismissively. "That's a long and not very interesting story."

"But I'm interested. In your story, I mean."

"It's nothing you need to know for the website."

"A romance gone wrong?" he guessed.

She sighed. "You don't give up, do you?"

"I'm sorry if I overstepped," he said, a little stiffly now. "It's an occupational hazard, I guess, needing to know all the details in order to solve a problem."

"And you think I'm a problem to be solved?"

"No. Of course not."

He glanced away, obviously flustered by her question—or maybe put off by the challenging tone of it.

And now she was sorry that she'd let an innocent question and uncomfortable memories put her on the defensive and destroy the comfortable rapport they'd begun to establish.

"In fact," he continued, "I think what you're doing here is amazing, Claire."

"I don't know if it's amazing, but it's necessary," she said.

"It's amazing," he said again. "And so are you."

She felt her heart swell inside her chest and had to remind herself to keep her distance.

"This would be an appropriate place for you to respond by saying something complimentary about me," he told her, a teasing note in his voice. "Something about me being a hottie, perhaps."

Right now, it was her cheeks that were hot.

Burning, in fact.

"I think I liked you better when you were tripping over your words, like you were on Monday," she remarked.

"So much for hoping you didn't notice."

"Maybe I shouldn't have mentioned it, but you're cute when you're flustered."

"*Cute* isn't nearly as flattering as *hottie*, but I'll take it," he decided.

"It's more than you deserve after eavesdropping on a private conversation," she said.

"You were having a private conversation…with your horse?"

"Next to Sarah, Crescent Moon is my oldest friend. And I implicitly trust both of them to keep my deepest secrets."

"And the fact that you think I'm a hottie is a deep secret?" He followed the question with a grin that made her knees wobble.

No more men. No more heartbreak.

"It was supposed to be a secret," she told him. "But since you did overhear that admission, I should probably clarify."

"I'm listening," he assured her.

"Yes, I think you're an incredibly attractive man, but I'm not looking for a relationship or a fling or anything else right now."

"Okay," he said easily.

She frowned. "That's it? You're not going to try to change my mind?"

"You sound pretty certain about what you want—and don't want," he noted. "Not like someone who's likely to change her mind."

"I am certain," she said, refusing to let any hint of *un*certainty creep into her tone.

"Then it would be a waste of both my time and yours

to try to change your mind, wouldn't it?" he said reasonably.

"Still, a woman likes to feel as if she's worth *some* effort," Claire grumbled.

"Right now, my efforts are focused on trying to decipher the mixed signals you're sending out."

"I'm sorry," she said, because he was right—she was sending out mixed signals when she hadn't intended to send out any signals at all. "Please forget I said anything."

"I can try, but I'm not likely to forget the hottie part."

He was teasing again, attempting to lighten the mood.

"I'm certain I'm not the first woman to describe you that way," she said, playing along.

"Maybe not," he acknowledged. "But you're for sure the prettiest."

She felt her cheeks flush again, but with pleasure this time.

"And further in the interest of clarity, I have no doubt that you'd be worth a lot of effort, but we need to work together to build your website, and I'm not sure that would be possible if I let myself pine over you."

"Pine over me?" she echoed, amused.

"I'm sure I wouldn't be the first man to do so."

She laughed then. "I think we're going to have to agree to disagree about that."

"So we'll work together," he said.

"And maybe…be friends?" she suggested.

He nodded slowly. "I'd like that."

"Good." She nodded, too. "You really aren't like any other guy I've ever met."

"Is that good or bad?" he wondered.

"I'm not entirely sure," she admitted.

But she was looking forward to figuring out the answer.

Do you ride?

Devin was still feeling slightly affronted by her question when they headed back to the barn.

Of course, tomorrow he'd probably be feeling more than slightly sore, because while he *could* ride—and quite well, thank you very much—it had been a long time since he'd been on the back of a horse.

Three or four months, probably. Perhaps even a little longer, but not as many as six. If it had been six months, Gramps would have been knocking on his door, demanding to know if he'd forgotten how to get to Crooked Creek.

Or maybe not, because Gramps had a lot of things to keep him busy these days. Not just helping Spencer care for the horses he trained, but a romance with Helen Powell. It was a sad but true fact of Devin's life that his eighty-year-old grandfather had more success with women than he did.

Not that it usually bothered him much. Truthfully, he was mostly too engrossed in his work to think about his lack of female companionship. But being with Claire Lamontagne had him thinking about it now. Being with Claire stirred desires that he'd ignored for a very long time. Desires that he'd have to ignore for a while longer, because she'd made it clear that she wasn't looking to get involved with anyone right now, and even if she was, she wouldn't choose someone like Devin.

Women like Claire Lamontagne never did.

Besides, she was a friend of Sarah's, he reminded himself.

But the reminder didn't stop him from appreciating how good she looked on the back of a horse. And standing on solid ground. And—

Damn. After only two meetings, he was already getting tangled up in knots over her.

As they drew close enough to see the barn, both Claire and Devin automatically slowed their horses to a walk, to cool them down. Once they were in the yard, they dismounted and loosened the cinches, then removed the tack, checking for any abrasions or sore spots.

"I not only know how to ride, I also know about appropriate after-ride care," he assured Claire, when he caught her glancing over at him again.

"Sorry," she said. "I've got a couple of less experienced riders who help out, and I usually have to go through the process, step by step, with them afterward."

"You don't have to apologize for looking after your horses," he assured her, as he moved his hands over the stallion's legs, checking for any signs of heat or swelling. "I just wanted to reassure you that I know what I'm doing."

She nodded. "I'll get the hose."

After the horses were hosed down and their hooves picked, they were turned out into the paddock.

"I see you've got one in solitary confinement," Devin

noted, his gaze on a severely underweight gelding grazing at the far side of a separate paddock.

"Bolt's only been here a couple of weeks and is still a little skittish yet," she said.

"You've taken on a lot of animals in a short period of time," he noted.

"Which proves that this area was in need of another horse rescue."

"So what's Bolt's story?"

"He was a tenth birthday present for a little boy who dreamed of being a cowboy, but the novelty of owning and caring for a horse quickly wore off."

"How did you find him?"

"Actually, Sarah's the one who told me about him. She had lunch with another friend from high school who sells real estate. When Missy toured the property to prepare the listing, she discovered the horse, essentially abandoned in a field."

"It's a shame that anyone who can write a check can buy a horse," he said.

"The owner could have been charged with animal neglect and cruelty," Claire noted. "But it was more important to me that he agreed to sign over the horse."

"Are you telling me that you personally went and knocked on his door?"

"It seemed like the most expedient course of action."

"And if he'd been antagonistic or violent? You must know that anyone who mistreats animals wouldn't hesitate to hurt a woman."

"Sarah knew where and when I was going," she told him.

"Oh well, then, at least the police would know where to start searching for your body."

She arched a brow. "Your cousin didn't mention that you were prone to melodrama."

"I'm not being melodramatic," he denied, irritated by her easy dismissal of his concerns though not entirely sure why. It was hardly any of his business how she conducted hers, but the idea that she'd deliberately risk her own safety for that of an animal made him admire the hell out of her at the same time he wanted to shake some sense into her.

He decided a change of topic was in order. "So... how long have you known Sarah?"

"Since kindergarten."

He shouldn't have been surprised by her response. If she'd grown up in Haven, it made sense that she would have met his cousin at school. What surprised Devin was that he didn't remember Claire, because although she would have been a couple grades behind him, their paths must have crossed at some point over the years.

Of course, he'd been even more introverted and socially awkward in high school than he was now, and the sight of a pretty girl would have given him heart palpitations, causing him to duck into the nearest room for cover. Still, he felt compelled to ask, "Did you go to Westmount?"

She nodded.

"I don't remember you," he admitted, and he was certain that he would have.

"We didn't exactly run with the same crowd."

No doubt because she was popular, and he was not.

"But I was well aware of your heartbreaker reputation," she told him.

"I think you mean my brother's reputation," he told her. "That was later attributed to me, too, simply because of our familial relationship."

"Are you saying that you didn't leave a trail of broken hearts in your wake?" she challenged.

"Not even a one," he assured her.

"I find that hard to believe."

"It's true," he insisted.

"Even if you didn't date as many girls as your brother during your four years at Westmount—"

"Three," he interjected, then felt like an idiot for doing so.

"What?"

He should have dropped the subject then. He should have shaken his head or waved it off in some other way. Instead, he heard himself say, "I fast-tracked through high school. Graduated after three years."

It's okay to be smarter than everyone else, because you don't really have any choice in that matter, Trevor had remarked to him—more than once over the years. But you don't have to point out to everyone you meet that you're smarter than them.

He shrugged then, but it was too late.

The damage was done.

He might as well walk around with a flashing Nerd Alert sign over his head.

"I guess you are every bit as smart as Sarah claims," Claire mused.

She sounded impressed rather than annoyed, although that was no doubt because she was interested in his computer science degree, not him. He'd be wise to remember that.

"My point is, even if you didn't date as much as your brother, and even if the girls had to track you down in the computer lab rather than on the football field, they still went after you."

He couldn't deny that was true, even if he rarely knew what to say to any of them when they found him.

"Because I'm a Blake," he said.

And they both knew that Blakes were akin to royalty in Haven.

"That was undoubtedly part of the reason," she acknowledged. "But I'd bet a bigger part is that you were sweet and shy and adorable."

Sweet and shy and adorable—definitely not words that had ever been ascribed to his brother.

Though the way Claire looked at him when she said those words did make them seem rather complimentary.

She glanced at her Fitbit then. "Yikes—is that the time?"

"If it says 1:55, it's probably the time. Otherwise, it might be your step count," he said.

"It says 1:55," she confirmed. "No wonder I'm hungry. Come on inside. We can talk about the website while I make lunch for us."

"You don't have to feed me," he protested.

"I know. But I'm hungry, so I figured you must be, too."

"I am," he admitted. "But—"

"Unless I'm taking up too much of your time," she said. "There are probably other places that you need to be."

"Not today."

"Then you might as well stay for lunch."

Chapter Five

She made it sound perfectly reasonable, and perhaps it was. And now that Claire had mentioned lunch, Devin was suddenly aware that he hadn't eaten anything since the bowl of Lucky Charms that was his breakfast more than five hours earlier.

"Thank you," he said, as he followed her into the house.

In the kitchen, she turned on the faucet, then soaped up her hands and rinsed them off.

"I cooked some chicken breasts yesterday—" she opened the fridge to retrieve a plate "—so I thought I'd make chicken salad sandwiches, if that sounds good."

"It sounds better than good," he assured her.

A jar of mayonnaise, celery, grapes and walnuts joined the chicken on the counter.

Following her example, Devin washed his hands in the sink and dried them on the same towel.

Claire was quick with the knife, he noted, having already cut the chicken into bite-size pieces and moved on to chopping the nuts.

She added them to the bowl with the chicken, then winced. "I meant to ask if you were allergic to nuts."

"No allergies," he told her.

"That's a relief," she said. "Or I would have been putting the chicken away and lighting the grill for burgers."

"You barbecue?" he asked, sounding surprised.

"It's the best way to cook burgers," she pointed out, slicing a stalk of celery down the middle. "And steak."

"You won't get any argument from me there," he said.

"So why did you sound surprised that I barbecue?"

"Because I fell into the trap of gender stereotypes," he admitted.

"Your mom cooks and your dad grills?" she guessed.

"Actually Greta cooks," he said. "I'm not sure my mother knows how to do anything more than boil the kettle to make tea—and she only makes her own tea when Greta isn't around.

"But yes, when we're having burgers or steak, it's usually my dad standing at the grill."

"It was the same at our house when I was growing up," she confided. "That's probably when I decided that I didn't ever want to depend on a man—or really anyone else—to do something for me." A slight smile tugged at the corners of her mouth. "Although I can't deny there are some activities that are much more enjoyable with a man's participation."

Devin felt heat creep up his neck as he realized she was talking about sex.

Thankfully, she didn't wait for him to respond, instead gesturing with the knife to the laptop on the table. "While I'm finishing up lunch, why don't you open up my computer and check out the tabs I've got open?"

He did as she suggested, frowning when he discovered that she didn't have any kind of password protection on her screen.

"You did some homework," he noted, as he clicked through the tabs.

"I thought it would be easier to show you other sites that appealed to me rather than try to explain what I want," she told him.

While he scanned the sites, she cut the grapes in half, then added a generous dollop of mayonnaise, a dash of salt and pepper, and a pinch of dried mustard to the bowl. He mentally catalogued the ingredients and steps of preparation, thinking he might try her recipe sometime at home.

Or maybe that was just an excuse to watch what she was doing.

Was it sexist that he found her ease in the kitchen an incredibly attractive trait?

He was capable of fending for himself at dinnertime—at least when he'd remembered to stock his fridge and pantry—but he wasn't particularly adventurous when it came to cooking. The truth was, he was more of a take-it-out-of-the-box-and-pop-it-into-the-microwave kind of guy.

"Can I help you with anything?" he asked, as she retrieved a loaf of bread from the box on the counter.

"You are," she said. "You're perusing my bookmarks to get an idea of how I want my website to look."

"Actually, I sent the links to myself so I can do a more thorough review of the sites at home."

"In that case, you can grab the pitcher of iced tea out of the fridge." She pointed to the cupboard over the sink. "Glasses are in there."

He poured two glasses of iced tea and set them on the table.

"I did take a quick glance at the sites, though," he said to her now. "And I'm curious about your selection of the Haven Animal Shelter site—it's a much more basic layout than the others you'd marked."

"Oh, that wasn't for you but for me," she admitted.

"You really are thinking about getting a dog?" he guessed.

"Aunt Susan and Uncle Mick always had one, sometimes two, but of course they took Holmes with them when they moved to California."

"Every ranch should have a dog," Devin agreed.

"I've just been so busy with other things, I haven't had a chance to visit the shelter. But when I was at The Trading Post the other day, I heard Brooke Stafford telling the cashier about a litter of puppies that were going to be available for adoption within the next couple of weeks."

"Everybody wants a puppy," Devin mused.

"Of course," she agreed. "Because they're adorable."

"They're also a lot more work than older dogs," he pointed out.

"I'd guess that depends on what kind of issues you might have to deal with in an older dog who's been rescued."

"That's a fair point," he acknowledged. "Although someone willing to take on a thousand-pound horse with issues wouldn't balk at doing the same for an animal a fraction of that size."

"Except that Twilight Valley is all about the horses, so they need to be the focus of my time and attention."

"It is a big project you've taken on," he noted. "Are you doing it all on your own or do you have a partner?"

"I'm primarily on my own, though in addition to the riders I mentioned earlier, there are a couple of teenage boys who live next door and who sometimes come over to help muck out stalls or feed the horses for community service hours, but I'm hoping the exposure of a website will bring in some dedicated volunteers.

"And sponsorships," she added. "Farm Feed & Supply is giving me a discount on grain and supplements, so I thought I should give them a mention on the website."

"That's a good idea," he agreed. "And it will attract other businesses who might want to offer some kind of sponsorship—whether money or goods or services."

"Money would be great," she said. "Right now I'm operating on a shoestring budget and hoping and praying that any or all of my grant applications will be approved."

"Is Twilight Valley a registered charity?"

She nodded.

"Then we can set up the site so that donations over a specified amount automatically generate tax receipts."

"You mean *you* can do that," she said.

"Huh?"

"You said *we* can set up the site," she explained. "And the reason you're here is that I don't have the first clue how to do anything like that."

"I thought the reason I was here is that you didn't want to trek into town again for another meeting you suspected I might forget."

"That, too," she agreed.

"But yes, *I* can set up the site to generate automatic tax receipts."

"But speaking of things that *I* can do—or hope that I can do," she said, circling the conversation back again. "Once the website is up, I'd like to be able to upload new images and bios when new horses come to the ranch and update the status of an animal who is successfully rehomed."

"You want to do the site updates?"

She nodded.

"Do you have any idea what that entails?"

"No," she admitted. "But I was hoping it would be something simple enough that you could show me."

"It would be simpler if you just provided me with whatever updated information you wanted to include so that I could do it," he told her.

"Just because I don't know how to build a website doesn't mean I'm a complete idiot," she told him, a defensive note slipping into her tone.

"I don't think you're any kind of idiot," he said. "I just figured you'd be too busy on the ranch to want to be bothered with such details."

"Oh."

But clearly someone had made her question her abilities and intelligence in the past.

"I apologize for jumping to conclusions, but I've had too many people tell me that I'm going to be way over my head with Twilight Valley and there's no way it's going to succeed."

"If your friends are telling you such things, you need new friends," he said bluntly.

"Not friends but family," she said. "And it isn't so easy to replace family."

"I'm sorry they're not being supportive."

She shrugged. "I didn't really expect my parents or brothers to approve of my choices—they never have before."

"I've got some experience with that, too," he confided.

"You're smart and successful—why would your family ever be disappointed in you?"

"Because I don't want to put on a tie and sit in an office every day and represent the next generation of Blake Mining."

"But you do work at Blake Mining."

"Only when I have to—otherwise, I work from home, mostly creating projects of my own or gaming."

"Gaming?"

Yep, there was that Nerd Alert sign flashing again;

because she was so easy to talk to, he didn't think to pause and censor his words.

"It shows me what types of games are currently popular, what makes them popular, what the user interface looks like, as well as giving me the opportunity to discover flaws so that they can be avoided in my own programming."

"What kind of games do you play?"

"Mostly MOBA-style games."

"MOBA?"

"Multiplayer online battle arena."

"Like *World of Warcraft*?"

He wasn't surprised by her question, because *WoW* seemed to be the one game that non-gamers knew the name of.

"Actually, *World of Warcraft* is an MMORPG—massively multiplayer online role-playing game," he told her. "But yes, I've spent some time exploring *World of Warcraft*."

"Did you ever have virtual sex with Glissinda the troll?"

Again, he was jarred by the casual mention of sex. Not because he was a prude, but because he wasn't accustomed to discussing such topics with beautiful women. Or discussing anything really with beautiful women.

Rather than answer her question—which would have been with a resounding *no*—he said, "You're a fan of *The Big Bang Theory*."

"Just don't tell my parents," she said.

Before he could question her about that cryptic remark, she moved on.

"As I already mentioned, I'm working on a pretty tight budget, so I'd like to know what this is going to cost before you put too much work into it and find out that I can't pay you for it."

"I'll give you the friends-and-family discount."

"Which still doesn't give me the slightest hint of a dollar amount," she pointed out.

"It won't be a lot," he promised.

She huffed out a breath. "You're being frustratingly vague."

"If you're concerned about the cost, maybe we could work out a trade."

Her eyes narrowed. "What did you have in mind?"

He realized he was treading on boggy ground. That a woman who looked like Claire had probably received her share of indecent proposals and was expecting another one now. But Devin really wasn't the kind of guy who would ever use sex as a bargaining chip.

"You could pay me in chicken salad sandwiches." He brushed the crumbs off his hands over the plate. "Because that was the best one I've ever had."

Her white-knuckle grip on her glass relaxed. "Let's see what you can do with my website first."

Claire watched Devin's Range Rover disappear down the driveway and out of sight, glad that she'd given him a second chance—and that she'd invited him out to the ranch. She'd enjoyed the time they'd spent together, and she'd been pleased to discover that, when he loosened up a little, he was easy to talk to.

She was still a little embarrassed that he'd overheard

her talking to Crescent Moon. And that she'd actually called him a hottie.

It wasn't a word she used very often, but it had seemed like a harmless admission to make, because she could trust the old mare not to share her secrets.

"Apparently it's my own big mouth that I need to worry about," she said now. "Or maybe I need to stop talking to animals."

A suggestion made, of course, to the animals.

"Or maybe it doesn't matter, because I probably won't see him again until he's finished with the website."

Now that they'd exchanged contact information, she imagined most of their communications going forward would be via email.

And that was a relief, because the very last thing she needed was to let herself be distracted from her responsibilities at Twilight Valley by an inconvenient and unwelcome attraction.

So why did the idea of not seeing him again leave her feeling vaguely disappointed?

Pushing all thoughts of Devin Blake aside, she turned away from the horses grazing in the paddock. As she did so, her attention was snagged by something fluttering in the breeze.

Devin's tie.

She picked it up and ran the silk through her fingers, smiling a little at the incomprehensible letters, numbers and symbols. Incomprehensible to her, anyway. No doubt they meant something to Devin.

She'd have to get the tie back to him, but for now, she

folded it carefully and tucked it into the front pocket of her jeans.

Back in the stables, she tidied up the already tidy tack room, checked her inventory of equipment and supplies, answered a few emails and sent a quick message to Devin to let him know that she had his tie. And found herself thinking again that the man looked damn good on the back of a horse. Definitely more cowboy than tech geek—and undeniably appealing.

No more men. No more heartbreak.

Because if she'd learned anything about herself since she'd climbed into the back seat of Jacob Nolan's Firebird a decade earlier, it was that she couldn't trust her own judgment about men.

How many times had she been in love?

More than she wanted to admit.

Of course, she hadn't been in love with Jacob and hadn't been foolish enough to think that she was. He'd meant nothing more to her than a means to an end, and she might have felt guilty about that if not for the fact that he'd also gotten exactly what he'd wanted from their back seat assignation.

But since then, she'd given her heart too readily to too many.

Now, faced with an unexpected attraction to Devin, she was having to remind herself of all the reasons she'd decided to take a break from romantic entanglements. And the number one reason was that she couldn't trust her own judgment when it came to personal relationships.

It would be safer and smarter to focus all of her time

and attention on the work she was doing at Twilight Valley, because that was something she knew she could feel good about. Because she was making a difference in the lives of the horses that came into her care for however long or short a period of time.

It pained her to see so much suffering—physical and emotional—in the animals. And it filled her with joy to be able to help—to be greeted by the whinny of a gelding that used to cower in the back of his stall whenever he heard footsteps drawing near, to brush the now glossy coat on the filly that had come in with severe skin irritation and hair loss as a result of an untreated lice infestation, to watch the mare that had suffered from laminitis trot happily around the paddock.

Was she trying to do good now to make up for being a bad girl in the past? For not being the daughter her parents deserved and the wife Eric wanted?

Maybe.

But at least now when people talked about her, they talked about Twilight Valley.

She was no longer the pastor's daughter being chased by all the boys trying to get into her pants. She was the woman in charge of the horse rescue, and if they didn't respect her, they at least respected the work she was doing.

It was a good enough start.

Devin had a lot to think about after his visit to Twilight Valley, and the website he needed to build was only a small part of what occupied his thoughts later that afternoon. Mostly he found himself thinking about Claire.

He was a problem-solver, but finding and fixing a bug in a line of code was infinitely easier than reading and understanding people—and women were the most incomprehensible of all people. Maybe it was because they always looked and smelled so good, and something about that combination never failed to short-circuit his brain.

Still, he thought he'd held his own pretty well today. There hadn't been any serious lags in the conversation and if he'd been startled to overhear her talking about him—and he was!—he'd managed to not only recover but later tease her about the remarks she'd made. Even more surprising, they'd found common ground in their connection to horses and their disconnect from their respective families.

More than once, his parents had expressed concern about his lack of ambition, and it had taken Devin a long time to realize that just because he didn't want the same things that they wanted for him didn't mean he was lazy. His disinterest in climbing the corporate ladder wasn't evidence of a lack of ambition, it was just proof that his ambitions lay elsewhere.

He appreciated all the opportunities that he'd been given at Blake Mining, but the family business wasn't his passion. What he loved was coding. The challenge of creating something magical and amazing out of nothing, or developing new and better ways to make things work.

And maybe he did spend a lot of his free time gaming—but wasn't free time supposed to be spent doing something you enjoyed?

Of course, he had a lot more free time these days, since his brother and now even several of his friends were married with kids. Family responsibilities inevitably changed the dynamic of outside relationships, and that was how it should be. It was part of the evolution of life, even if it wasn't the evolution he'd necessarily envisioned for his own.

But maybe, if someone like Claire Lamontagne actually thought he was a hottie, he might have to reimagine his future. Consider the possibility that he might someday meet a woman—not someone like Claire, of course, he still had to be realistic—fall in love and get married.

Because the more time he spent with Trevor and Haylee and Aidan and Ellie, the more he wanted what his brother and sister-in-law had. And the more he realized that he was a fifth wheel to their family unit.

Notification of a message popped up on his screen, interrupting his musing.

Cnfrnc nxt wknd in LAS—wnna cnnct?

Even if he hadn't known by the screen name—LT98—that it was one of his online teammates, her aversion to spelling out words would have given her away. She was like a *Wheel of Fortune* contestant who couldn't afford to buy a vowel, which he thought was funny, because her full name—Laura Wojciechowsky—contained every one of them.

This wasn't the first time she'd propositioned him. Or even the second or the third. Although her home base was in Colorado, she traveled frequently to Nevada and California for business—and pleasure. Like Devin—and most of their online group—she spent the majority of her days alone. During another long-ago private chat, she'd confided to him that she'd had a few relationships, but none that had lasted very long and she'd decided that hookups were a lot more fun and a lot less work than dating.

Sorry. *(Not.)* I'm in the middle of a big project *(total lie)* and will probably be working all weekend.

Tht scks. Lng dry spll—nd 2 gt ld.

He wasn't quite sure how to respond.
Good luck with that?
Enjoy your weekend?
You think you're *in a dry spell?*
Definitely not the latter—because he had no desire to prolong the conversation and give Laura the least bit of encouragement.
Instead, he settled for quoting the tourism slogan.

What happens in Vegas, stays in Vegas.

U knw it! ;)

He opened up his email and clicked on the links that he'd sent to himself from Claire's computer.

As he was perusing the first website, a new email message came through—from Claire.

He immediately switched tabs to scan the brief message.

I found your tie—thankfully before Lily and Daisy did. I'll drop it off to you the next time I'm in town.

He replied:

I've got some errands to run in the morning, so I'll swing by to pick it up, if you're going to be around.

I'll be here.

As he turned his attention back to the website, he realized that, in the space of five minutes, he'd lied twice to different women. First, in making an excuse *not* to see Laura and second, in fabricating a reason to see Claire.

And he didn't feel guilty about either one.

Chapter Six

Claire had been wrong in thinking that she wouldn't see Devin again until he was finished with her website. He showed up the very next day, as he'd indicated in his email, arriving just as Jasmine was being unloaded from her trailer after an arduous journey from Twin Falls. Then he'd made another trip to Twilight Valley the day after that, to see how the broodmare was adjusting to her new home, and another two days later.

Claire should have been annoyed by the almost daily interruptions, except for the fact that Devin didn't take her away from her work but actually pitched in to help. And unlike some of her volunteers, who had more enthusiasm than experience, he knew what he was doing. She didn't have to show him how to use a currycomb or explain the feeding chart or warn him not to stand behind a horse. Which, unfortunately, also meant that she didn't have an excuse to stick close to him.

Because despite having sworn off men, she liked spending time with Devin. And she'd gotten so used to seeing him around, that if more than three days passed without him visiting the ranch, she missed him.

"What's going on with you?"

The impatient tone of Sarah's question snapped Claire back to the present. "What?"

Her friend rolled her eyes. "That's what I want to know. You've been distracted all morning. We've been here—"

She glanced around, looking for a clock, but Serenity Spa promoted the idea of escapism from the real world, which meant that there were no clocks—only watercolor paintings and inspirational sayings on the walls.

"—almost three hours," Sarah guesstimated, "and you've been distracted the whole time."

"I've been relaxing," Claire said. "Isn't that why we're here?"

It wasn't Vegas, but the hot stone massages followed by mani-pedis were a welcome indulgence for both of them.

Though Claire had protested that a manicure would be wasted on her, Sarah insisted that a manicure was about hand and nail care even more than color. Claire had remained dubious, but she had to admit that her hands felt really good after the luxurious paraffin wax treatment.

Still, she'd declined the offer of polish for her fingernails, knowing it wouldn't survive even a day in the stables. Her toes were a different matter, though. Even if no one else ever saw her feet because they were in boots most of the time, she liked to see the color on her toes when she went barefoot in the house.

"You've been distracted," Sarah insisted.

"Maybe a little," she admitted. "I've just got a lot on my mind."

"A lot?" Sarah challenged. "Or a man?"

"I swore off men," she reminded her friend.

"And yet."

"And yet," she agreed, with a sigh.

"Are you going to tell me who it is—or are you going to make me guess?"

Claire wiggled her toes, freshly painted Strawberry Margarita. "There's nothing to know, really, because nothing's going to happen."

"Not every guy you meet is going to be like Eric," Sarah said.

She knew her friend was trying to be reassuring, but before Eric there had been Bryan, Steve, Gord, Christopher and Vince—and a few others—and none of those relationships had worked out. All of which had led Claire to the inescapable conclusion that they weren't the problem, *she* was.

"In fact, there are plenty of great guys out there. Like my cousin Devin, for example," she continued.

Claire felt her face flush so that it was probably as pink as her toes. "Please tell me it's not obvious that I'm crushing on your cousin."

"It wouldn't be obvious to anyone but me."

Her gaze narrowed on the smug expression on her friend's face. "Ohmygod—you set us up."

"Hardly," Sarah scoffed.

"You did," Claire insisted, convinced now that it was true. And wondering why she hadn't suspected something from the beginning.

I can't believe you don't have a website.

One of my cousins is a whiz with computers—he could do it.

Let me make a call, set up a meeting.

"The website was your idea," she suddenly remembered.

"Because every business needs a website," Sarah said reasonably.

And okay, that was true. And it was something Claire would have thought of herself if she hadn't been so preoccupied with other aspects of the business.

"And then you told me that Devin could build it," she pointed out.

"Because he can," came the logical reply.

But Claire wouldn't let herself be fooled by her friend's deliberate nonchalance for another minute.

"Do you really expect me to believe that you had no ulterior motives?" she challenged.

"Maybe I considered the possibility that you and he might hit it off," Sarah finally conceded.

"You set us up," Claire said again.

"And if there had been no chemistry between you, that would have been the beginning and end of it."

Another undeniable truth, she admitted, if only to herself.

"Which makes me think there's some chemistry there," her friend mused.

"There might be," Claire allowed.

"Serious chemistry?" Sarah pressed, sounding hopeful.

She sighed. "I thought so, but…he hasn't made a move."

Her friend frowned. "I know Devin can be shy, but I didn't think he was obtuse." She sipped her cucumber water. "What aren't you telling me?"

That was the thing about best friends—they always knew when you weren't being completely forthright.

"Well…way back in the beginning—" which was admittedly only two weeks earlier "—I might have told him that I wasn't looking to get involved."

"Might have?"

"Okay, *did* tell," she acknowledged.

"And now you're upset that he's respecting your wishes?" Sarah didn't try to hide her amusement.

"But that was weeks ago, before I really knew him."

"Uh-huh."

"Okay, I'm being ridiculous," she admitted.

"Uh-huh," her friend said again.

"So what am I supposed to do now?"

"If you want something to happen, you're going to have to tell him that you changed your mind."

"And that's the real dilemma," she confided. "Because I'm not sure I have. I mean, I *like* Devin. He's handsome and sweet and charming, and he really does seem like one of the good guys."

"I'm not seeing a dilemma," Sarah told her.

"Sometimes I watch him with the horses, and the way he handles them—he's so confident and strong that I almost ache with wanting to feel his hands on me."

Sarah fanned herself dramatically. "Forget telling him anything—why haven't you made a move?"

"Because then I remember that he's your cousin."

"We've been best friends forever," Sarah noted. "But thinking about me in the midst of your sexual fantasies about my cousin is a little weird."

"I don't think of you in the midst of sexual fantasies about your cousin. I'm not having sexual fantasies about your cousin," she denied. "I never let my mind wander too far in that direction because he *is* your cousin, and if something were to happen between me and Devin and one of us ended up heartbroken—because, let's be honest, someone *always* ends up heartbroken—things would be awkward between you and me."

"Someone doesn't *always* end up heartbroken," Sarah protested. "In just the last few years, all four of my Channing cousins fell in love, got married and added—" she paused to do a quick calculation on her fingers "—six kids to the family. My brother Patrick fell in love with Brooke, and now they're happily married with a little brother or sister on the way for Brendan, and Devin's brother married Haylee Gilmore only a few months before welcoming twins to their family."

"Apparently your family is solely responsible for Haven's recent baby boom," Claire noted.

"My point is, if you'd take a minute to look past your cynicism, you'd see that love is all around you."

"Please don't break into song."

"I'm not going to break into song," Sarah promised. "And now that song is going to be stuck in my head for the rest of the day—but it's a good song."

"It is a good song," Claire agreed. "And I'm happy for all your cousins and your brother and Devin's brother, but their collective happiness doesn't negate my history of heartache and I'm not willing to chance another one."

"So maybe you're not as over Eric as you want to believe."

"I'm definitely over Eric."

"Then prove it," her friend challenged. "Prove it by giving Devin a chance."

Claire didn't need to prove to Sarah that she was over Eric, because she knew that she was. Not wanting to get involved in another relationship wasn't evidence that she had lingering feelings for her ex. On the contrary, she took it as proof that she'd finally learned from the mistakes of her past. So while she wasn't ready to take a chance on a man, she decided that maybe it was time to take a chance on a dog.

Haven Animal Shelter was housed in a spacious and clean building, staffed by dedicated workers and enthusiastic volunteers. To ensure that she didn't make any impulsive decisions, Claire promised herself that today's visit would just be a reconnaissance mission—to see what kinds of dogs were currently available and if any seemed like a good fit for the ranch.

I'm not going home with a dog today.

She repeated the words to herself as she walked through the automatic doors.

Or a puppy, she quickly added, just in case she was tempted to wriggle out of the promise on a technicality.

Because ever since she'd heard Brooke mention those puppies, the idea of bringing one of them home had sprouted in her mind, rooting a little deeper every day.

She'd checked the website regularly, waiting for the puppies to be added to the "Dogs Available for Adoption" page, and then they finally were. According to the site, mom was a yellow lab and dad was a beagle, and while Claire couldn't imagine how *that* mating had happened, there was no denying that the six puppies—four girls and two boys—were absolutely adorable.

She had enough to do around the ranch to keep her busy throughout the day. Word had spread around town about what she was doing at the Cartwright Ranch (because, in the way of small close-knit communities, Twilight Valley would likely forever remain known to many of the locals by its former title), so it was rare that a day passed without someone stopping by. Some were just being nosey—wanting to see what the pastor's errant daughter was up to on her horse ranch. Others were sincerely interested and some of them even offered to help.

Claire wasn't foolish enough to turn down the offer of free labor. Now she had a handful of regular volunteers and a greater number who showed up on a less frequent schedule to lend a hand. Of course, she was the primary caregiver of all the equine residents of Twilight Valley, but it was important for the horses to get used to new and different people if she was going to be successful in rehoming them.

So while her days were generally full, at night, the

big house was empty and quiet. She didn't mind living alone, but she thought it might be nice to have some companionship. And since she didn't envision a romantic relationship anywhere in her future—*No more men. No more heartbreak.*—she thought a dog would be good company.

It wasn't difficult to find the puppies. While most dogs were housed in separate kennels, the six little ones were kept together in the largest enclosure on the end, with glass on three sides. And on all three sides, prospective adopters stood shoulder to shoulder, watching the puppies play—climbing over their siblings, chewing on ears and chasing tails.

A volunteer whose name tag identified her as Bonnie handed Claire a clipboard with an adoption application attached.

"Successful applicants will be contacted by the end of the week and the puppies will be available to go home with their new families next Saturday." Her monotone indicated that she'd imparted the same information countless times already and expected to repeat it countless times again.

When Claire had walked through the doors, she'd been certain that she wanted a puppy—even if she wasn't going to take one home today—but now that she was here, surrounded by so many others wanting the same thing, she found herself moving past the puppy enclosure to look at the other dogs available for adoption.

Each kennel had an information sheet taped to the glass that provided some basic details about the dog inside—including name, breed, age (or an approximation), personality traits, and health and behavioral issues, if any.

Ivan was an eight-year-old Chihuahua with big eyes and bigger ears who was found abandoned. He was cute and energetic—and he wouldn't take up much space in her bed—but Claire suspected that a little dog like that might get lost—or hurt—on the ranch.

Celia was a two-and-a-half-year-old cocker spaniel with silky black fur whose owners had surrendered her because they were moving out of the country. There was also a smiley face sticker on her page with the notation I'm Adopted.

Durango was a four-year-old Great Pyrenees that suffered from separation anxiety and would do best with a family that could give him lots of attention and long daily walks. But his kennel was currently empty, and Claire suspected that the huge fluffy white dog she'd seen in the Meet & Greet area outside was likely Durango.

And then there was Ed—a five-year-old Shollie— German shepherd/collie mix—also in the shelter as a result of owner surrender. His coat was primarily tan and white with numerous splotches of black. He was beautiful and big—but not too big—and, it seemed to Claire, more than a little sad.

Maybe that was an odd emotion to ascribe to a dog, but while the other dogs eagerly came over to the glass when she stopped by their enclosures, as if to say "pick me," Ed didn't even lift his head from its resting place on top of a sparkly pink stuffed unicorn toy. But when she didn't immediately move on, he did open one eye to peer at her with what looked like wariness rather than interest.

She squatted so that she was closer to his level, and his tail swished over the floor.

Once. Twice.

"How are you doing, Ed?"

She wasn't sure how much he could hear through the glass, but his ears twitched then, and the second eye opened to give her a more thorough appraisal.

"It must be hard to sleep, with so many people coming and going, fussing over the puppies, huh?"

He rose to his feet then and padded the short distance to the glass, pressing his nose right against it, making her smile.

She lifted her hand and splayed her palm on the other side of the barrier. "I'm Claire," she said. "I live on a ranch just outside of town."

He cocked his head to the side, as if trying to decipher her humanspeak.

"Do you like horses? Goats?"

His head twisted to the other side.

She smiled. "I can't take you home today, because I'm trying to be less emotional and impulsive in my decision-making—although still apparently talking to animals."

Ed's tail swished again.

"But let's see if we can't get to know one another a little better without this pane of glass between us, okay?"

She stepped away from the kennel then, to seek out

one of the shelter workers, and Ed went back to his unicorn.

Claire found Bonnie sitting behind a desk, reviewing a stack of adoption applications.

"Busy place today," Claire noted.

"It's been like this since we put the puppies on the website, and it will be like this until next Saturday, when they've all been adopted."

"If you can spare a few minutes, I was hoping to meet Ed."

"I can," Bonnie said. "Ryan is dealing with the puppy crowd right now and Kelly's answering questions in the cat corner." She tucked the applications into a drawer and pushed away from her desk. "I'm sorry—did you say you wanted to meet…Ed?"

Had Claire misread his name on the card?

"The German shepherd/collie mix with the stuffed pink unicorn."

"That's Ed," Bonnie confirmed. "I was just…surprised. He's been here with us for almost five months and none of our previous visitors has shown any particular interest in him."

"Why not?" Claire asked, immediately wary. "Does he have behavioral problems or health issues that aren't noted on his card?"

"No," the volunteer was quick to assure her. "It's just that most adopters want a younger dog—preferably a puppy."

"I came in to see the puppies," Claire confided. "But there's just something about Ed that tugged at my heart."

"He's a sweet dog," Bonnie said. "Even-tempered and good-natured."

"I have no intention of going home with a dog today," Claire said, wanting to be clear about that—and perhaps to remind herself. "But I've filled out an application—" she held up the clipboard "—so if there's nothing about him—or me—standing in the way, Ed's the one I'd like to meet."

"Of course," Bonnie agreed. "Do you know where the Meet & Greet area is?"

She nodded. "I passed it on the way in."

"Why don't you go ahead and grab a seat at one of the picnic tables, and I'll bring Ed out to meet you?"

She didn't have to wait long for Bonnie and Ed to join her, though the dog seemed much less excited about being outside than his handler.

Maybe he was just shy, but Claire couldn't shake the feeling that he was sad. Perhaps missing the owner who'd surrendered him and the home he used to know.

She could see the loss and grief in his eyes.

But she saw something else, too. Something she'd seen in some of the horses she'd taken in.

Something she recognized as cautious hope.

She sat still, waiting for the dog to approach her.

He paused a few feet away and plunked his butt down on the grass, as if he was willing to meet her halfway but would go no farther.

"It's okay," Bonnie said to the dog. "Claire's a friend."

Claire was surprised by the woman's use of her

name, then realized she must have read it on her application.

But despite Bonnie's reassurance, Ed refused to budge.

"He's a sweet dog," she said again. "But stubborn, too."

"Is it okay if I approach him?"

Bonnie nodded.

Claire lowered herself onto the grass, then shifted a little closer to the dog.

Ed held still, eyeing her warily.

"You weren't so shy behind the glass," she noted. "But maybe that's your safe space."

She leaned back on her elbows and stretched her legs, so that he'd know she wasn't a threat.

He crept a little closer, deigning to sniff her boots and the cuffs of her jeans.

"I live on a ranch," Claire told Bonnie. "He's probably smelling horses and goats and barn cats."

"Then you've got lots of space for a dog to run around, though Ed is very much an indoor dog."

"That's what I'm looking for," she agreed, then hastened to add, "But not today."

Bonnie smiled. "I'm not going to try to change your mind. In fact, I wish more people would take the time to consider the commitment they're making before they come in to select a pet."

"His bio said owner surrender," Claire remembered, holding back a smile as Ed inched a little bit closer. "Can you tell me why his owner gave him up?"

"In this case, yes," the volunteer said. "Ed previously

lived with an elderly widow who moved into an assisted care facility about eight months ago. Joyce's daughter, understanding how much her mom loved Ed, took him home with her, not realizing that her husband had severe allergies. He tried to manage them with medication, but not very successfully, so Nina finally, reluctantly, brought Ed here."

"No wonder he looks sad," Claire remarked.

Even the secondhand account of his ordeal was enough to tug at her heartstrings.

"He does seem a little melancholy sometimes," Bonnie agreed. "Especially in the days immediately after one of his friends here is adopted. Blossom and Durango were his most recent dog park buddies, but Blossom went home with her new family this morning, and Durango's prospects are looking good, too."

Ed nudged her thigh with his nose, and she scratched the soft fur beneath his chin. "I imagine, in five months, he's seen a fair number of friends go."

"He has, indeed."

"I know we're not friends yet," Claire said to the dog. "But I'm going to come back to see you tomorrow, okay?"

Ed gave a half-hearted wag of his tail, as if he might look forward to seeing her again but didn't entirely trust that he would.

"He'll be here," Bonnie promised.

Chapter Seven

But he wasn't.

When Claire returned to Haven Animal Shelter the following afternoon, Ed's enclosure was empty.

"Is Bonnie here?" she asked another volunteer—Maureen, according to the ID on the lanyard around her neck.

Maureen shook her head. "Bonnie doesn't work on Wednesdays. Is there something I can help you with?"

"I was here yesterday, visiting with Ed, and I told Bonnie that I'd come back today, but Ed's gone." Claire's voice sounded frantic even to her own ears, and she wasn't sure why.

Wouldn't it be a good thing if someone else had come in and adopted the dog? Because that would mean Ed already had a new home, maybe even a whole family with kids who'd throw a ball for him to fetch and tug on the other end of a knotted rope and drop scraps of food from the table.

And there were plenty of other dogs who would be happy at Twilight Valley, she knew. But for some reason, she'd set her heart on Ed and now—

"He'll be back—" Maureen glanced at the clock on the wall "—in about an hour."

"He wasn't adopted?"

The volunteer shook her head sadly. "Not yet. On the first Wednesday of every month, one of our dog walkers takes him to Shady Pines to visit his former owner."

Claire exhaled a sigh of relief. "Is that something an adopter would be asked to continue?"

"Oh, no," Maureen said. "I'm sure, once Ed is settled into a new home, he'll forget about his visits to Shady Pines."

Claire wasn't so sure. "What about his former owner?"

"Unfortunately, Joyce has forgotten about Ed already. She lights up when she sees him, because she's always been a dog lover, but she doesn't remember that Ed was her dog."

"That's sad," Claire said.

"It is," Maureen agreed. "It will be even sadder if Ed doesn't find a new home. I expected that David—he's the volunteer dog walker—would have taken him home before now, but he insists that Ed deserves to be with someone who can give him more attention than he can."

"I can't stay until Ed gets back," Claire said regretfully, because there was an order waiting at the feed store that she needed to pick up before she was due at her parents' house for dinner, and dinner was always served at precisely five o'clock.

"No worries," Maureen assured her.

But Claire *was* worried. Because she'd promised Ed that she would see him today, and now she wasn't going to. And maybe it was silly to be concerned about breaking a promise she'd made to a dog, but she wanted Ed to know that he could count on her.

"Will you tell him that Claire was here and that I'll come back tomorrow?"

"Sure thing," the volunteer readily agreed.

And Claire knew that she would be back.

Because contrary to her best efforts, she'd fallen in love again—this time with a four-legged creature who maybe needed her as much as she needed him.

If Claire stopped at Sweet Caroline's—as she'd planned to do when she left the feed store—she was going to be late.

But she believed that showing up a few minutes late with dessert was better than being on time and empty-handed. And luck seemed to be on her side when a vehicle pulled out of a parking spot right in front of the bakery, allowing her to zip into the now vacant slot.

Because it was late in the afternoon, there was only one employee behind the counter—and one customer ahead of her. The server looked vaguely familiar to Claire, so she guessed the young woman was someone she'd gone to school with, though obviously not part of her core group of friends. The customer was familiar, too. Though Claire was staring at his back, she recognized him not only by his height and his shape but by the familiar tug she felt low in her belly whenever she was in close proximity to the man.

She took a step closer to the counter, and Devin glanced over his shoulder, a smile of recognition curving his lips.

"You're a long way from home," he remarked.

"I'm headed to my parents' house for dinner," she explained. "I usually take dessert."

"If you want to score extra points, go for the apple caramel cheesecake."

"My mom's not a fan of cheesecake," she told him. "But she does like doughnuts."

The server finished making Devin's coffee and set it on the counter. "Can I get you anything else?"

"Actually, a doughnut sounds good," he said.

While Devin surveyed the treats in the display case, Claire did the same, breathing a sigh of relief to discover that there was one apple fritter left.

The server reached for a plate and a pair of tongs.

"Give me the apple fritter," he decided.

"No!"

Devin and the server both turned to Claire.

"Go for a chocolate glazed," she urged him. "Or a vanilla dip. I'll even buy your coffee and your doughnut—so long as it's not the apple fritter."

"Your mom's favorite?" he guessed, sounding amused.

"My dad's," she confided.

"I guess I'll go for a chocolate glazed," he told the server.

She transferred the requested pastry to the plate, then set the plate on the counter beside his coffee.

He pulled out his wallet.

"No," Claire said again, though less forcefully this time. "Let me get it."

"That's really not necessary," he told her.

"Please," she said.

He shrugged and tucked his wallet back into his pocket. "Thank you."

"Thank *you* for giving up the last apple fritter." Then to the server waiting for her order she said, "I'll take half a dozen doughnuts, starting with the apple fritter."

The server reached for a box and began to fill it with Claire's additional requests: lemon-filled, glazed twist, sugared twist, toasted coconut and Boston cream.

"Do you have time to join me for a coffee?" Devin asked, as she passed her money across the counter.

"Unfortunately, I don't," she said, with sincere regret. "I'm already going to be late."

"Maybe another time?" he suggested, perhaps a little tentatively.

She held his gaze for just a moment, just long enough to confirm that there was something happening between them—if she was willing to let it.

"I'd like that," she told him.

And maybe it was a mistake to encourage him—and herself—but she walked out of the bakery with her box of doughnuts in hand already looking forward to the next time that she'd see him again.

* * *

"It's been a long time since we've just hung out, watching a game together," Trevor remarked, accepting the bottle of beer his brother offered.

"Well, you've been a little busy with the whole wife-and-kids thing," Devin acknowledged.

"Yeah." Trevor grinned. "Life has been good."

"Toddlers throwing up on your ties notwithstanding?"

"If I'm being perfectly honest, baby vomit and dirty diapers aren't my favorite parts of fatherhood, but there's so much good stuff that tips the scales in the other direction. And then, of course, there's Haylee."

"Who cleans up the baby vomit and dirty diapers?" Devin asked dryly.

"Hey, I do my share," Trevor protested. "And Haylee does so much more than take care of the babies."

"I really don't want to hear about what goes on in your bedroom."

"I wasn't going to tell you," his brother assured him. "Because that wasn't what I meant, either. Although the endorphins released during lovemaking do wonders for the mind and body—you should try it sometime."

"You know, I remember when we used to watch a ballgame and. Actually. Watch. The. Ballgame," Devin said.

"The Yankees are having a conference on the mound in anticipation of a pitching change—there's nothing to see right now."

A valid point, Devin had to admit, as he tipped his bottle to his lips and swallowed a mouthful of beer.

"Seriously, Dev, you've been in a prickly mood for a while now. When was the last time you got laid?"

"I'm not in a prickly mood."

Unfortunately, the instinctive denial was weakened by the fact that he sounded, well, prickly.

"I've just got a lot on my plate right now."

Trevor seemed to accept that response more readily.

"Are you still working on that website for Sarah's friend?"

"Yeah."

"I know websites aren't your favorite thing, but it doesn't usually take you this long to put one together."

"Like I said, I've got a lot on my plate right now."

"If you want to be working instead of watching the game, just say so. I can sit in front of the TV at home instead of here."

"Your wife kicked you out," Devin reminded him.

"She didn't kick me out," Trevor denied hotly. "She simply suggested that I could spend some time with my brother while she was hanging out with her sister."

Devin knew that Haylee had always been close with Finley, and that the two sisters had remained so despite the geographical distance that separated them now that Haylee lived in Haven. And though Finley had a thriving business as an event planner in Oakland, she took advantage of any break in her schedule to visit her sister and dote on her niece and nephew.

"Anyway, I didn't plan on working tonight," Devin said to his brother now. Because he wasn't sure he'd be able to concentrate on anything more demanding

than the baseball game after his chance encounter with
Claire at the bakery.

I'd like that, she'd said, when he suggested they
might get together another time.

And though it was one of those things that people
often said without really meaning it, he'd gotten the impression that her response had been sincere.

"Maybe you should," Trevor said, drawing his attention back to the present. "Get the website done and
get it off your plate."

"Yeah, I'll probably do that this weekend."

"Or maybe you're not really eager to finish it," Trevor
mused. "Because as soon as the website's done, you
won't have any reason to see the hot horse whisperer."

"Her name's Claire," he reminded his brother. "And
that's ridiculous."

But also quite possibly true, Devin acknowledged.

There was no reason that he shouldn't have been able
to put together a website by now. Instead, he kept making excuses to trek out to Twilight Valley, to get more
information or take more pictures, to be there when
Toby left the ranch to enjoy his final years as a companion to Nigel Walker's aging stallion.

Claire had been smiling as she waved goodbye when
the rancher drove away, and though her eyes were hid-
den behind the dark lenses of her sunglasses, he'd
caught the telltale shimmer of tears on her cheeks.

The tears had tugged at something inside him, and
without conscious thought, he'd lifted a hand and gently
brushed them away.

"He was my first rescue," she'd confided, with just

the slightest hint of a tremor in her voice. "Almost sent to slaughter just because he was old, so I knew he'd be a fairly easy one to rehome—I just had to find the right home for him."

She'd obviously been sad to let the horse go, but she'd done so because she knew it was the best thing for Toby. It was that combination of softness and strength that had hooked Devin even more than her striking beauty, sexy body and sassy smile.

She was, to his mind, everything he could ever imagine wanting in a woman.

And everything he knew he could never have.

So the smart thing to do would be to finish up the website and then put Twilight Valley and Claire out of his mind.

But for the first time in his life, Devin didn't want to do the smart thing—he wanted to be with Claire.

"You got a dog." They were the first words out of Sarah's mouth when she saw her friend sitting on the porch with Ed by her side.

Claire grinned. "I got a dog."

She'd returned to the shelter on Thursday and signed the papers to officially adopt Ed, then clipped the leash she'd bought onto his collar.

The staff had all gathered round to see him off, and Bonnie rang the ceremonial bell that symbolized a shelter animal was going to its forever home. It was a sound Ed had likely heard hundreds of times before, and several of the employees and volunteers had been misty-eyed to hear it finally being rung for Ed.

As Sarah made her way toward them, Ed pressed closer to Claire's side. She hadn't been sure how he'd respond to new people, so she'd lured her friend to the ranch with the promise of wine and cheese and conversation.

Of course, Sarah didn't really need to be lured. Claire only needed to ask and her best friend would be there in a heartbeat, so the wine and cheese were really more of a celebration in honor of her new canine companion.

Sarah had obviously come straight from work as she was wearing a sheath-style dress topped with a little bolero jacket and three-inch heels on her feet that didn't even wobble as she picked her way across the gravel drive.

"What's her name?" Sarah asked, as she drew nearer.

"*His* name is Ed," Claire told her.

Sarah wrinkled her nose. "What kind of a name is Ed for a dog?"

"The one he came with."

"He's so handsome," she said. "Too handsome to be stuck with such an uninspired name."

Claire rolled her eyes.

"I'll call him Eduardo," Sarah decided. "What do you think, Eduardo? Doesn't that suit you better?"

Ed lifted a paw.

Charmed by the animal's gesture, Sarah dropped to her knees and took his paw in her hand to shake.

"You're going to get your dress dirty," Claire protested.

"It'll wash," her friend said dismissively, releasing the dog's paw to stroke his silky fur.

"You mean your dry cleaner will wash it."

"Same thing." She was still focused on the dog, already half in love. "I've been kicking myself for almost two years for not snatching up one of Princess's puppies when I had the chance."

"Princess...your brother's dog?"

Sarah nodded. "She's a beautiful doodle. And I'll bet that Princess and Eduardo would have made gorgeous puppies together, except that Brooke made sure Princess's first litter of puppies was also her last."

"And Ed's fixed, too," Claire said.

"Oh well. I'm not really home enough for a dog, anyway," she said. "So I guess I'll just have to get my doggy fix by visiting the Silver Star or Twilight Valley."

"You know you're welcome anytime."

"I also know that I was promised wine," Sarah said.

"And you will get wine," Claire promised. "Do you want it here or inside?"

"It's a nice evening—let's sit out for a while."

So they sat on the porch, nibbling on crackers and cheese and sipping a nice Riesling from Washington State while Claire told Sarah about her trip to the animal shelter and the search for a puppy that ended up with her finding Ed.

"I think you lucked out," Sarah said. "Eduardo is obviously as smart as he is handsome."

"He does seem to understand all the basic commands."

"And he knows how to shake a paw."

"And, most important, he's housebroken."

"That's a major bonus," Sarah agreed.

"I think he's going to be happy here."

"Of course he's going to be happy here." Sarah gestured to the fields and stables. "This is doggy heaven on earth."

Claire laughed softly. "I don't know that it's all that, but he's certainly got room to roam and other animals to make friends with—although so far he's very cautious of Lily and Daisy."

"He probably hasn't come across too many goats in his lifetime."

"Probably not," Claire agreed.

"How is he with the horses?"

"I'd say curious but cautious. Actually, that's a pretty accurate description of his demeanor in general since I brought him home. It's almost as if he doesn't want to get too comfortable because he doesn't trust that I'm going to keep him."

"Who can blame him for having doubts? From what you told me, in the past eight months he's lost his home and the woman who's cared for him since he was a puppy, then he was taken to another home, but he only lived there for a few months before he ended up at the shelter."

"I guess it does make sense for him to be wary," Claire agreed. "It's just that I bought all this stuff for him—a memory foam dog bed, stainless steel bowls for food and water, a new collar and leash and various toys and treats. And last night, he still went to sleep on the floor, cuddled up with his pink unicorn."

"You bought Eduardo a pink unicorn?"

"No, Ed brought the unicorn with him from the shelter."

And the dog knew exactly what they were talking about, because he went to the door to be let inside, and came back less than a minute later with the stuffed toy in his mouth.

Sarah laughed. "It's not just pink, but sparkly." She picked up the toy when Ed dropped it in her lap. "And slimy."

"And his favorite thing in the world, apparently."

"Because it's familiar," Sarah said. "But I'm sure it won't be too long before you're his favorite thing in the world."

She turned her attention back to the dog. "Do you want this—" she held up the toy, dangling it between her thumb and forefinger "—or this?" She showed him a piece of cheese.

He plopped on his butt, his gaze fixed on the cheese.

"Don't give him—"

But it was too late. Sarah had already offered the cheese and Ed had gulped it down.

"—cheese," she finished anyway.

Sarah looked stricken. "Why can't he have cheese? Don't all dogs love cheese?"

"Apparently he does, too," Claire observed. "But they warned me at the shelter that he's lactose intolerant— that dairy products give him gas."

"Oh." Her friend exhaled an obvious sigh of relief. "I was worried that he might have some kind of serious reaction."

Fifteen minutes later, they discovered that Ed's gas

was a serious reaction. In fact, it smelled so bad that even the dog ran away from it, which made both Claire and Sarah laugh even while they were gagging.

"Despite that stink bomb, I'm happy to know that you invited me to come over to meet Ed," Sarah said, when the smell had finally dissipated. "I was a little concerned that there might have been a blowup when you had dinner with your parents the other night."

"No blowup," she assured her friend.

"So how was dinner?"

"It was…fine."

Sarah arched her brows.

"No, really, it was. The meal was good, conversation was mostly pleasant."

"Mostly pleasant," her friend echoed, wrinkling her nose.

Claire sighed. "I guess I just thought—or at least hoped—that they would have forgiven me by now."

"You didn't do anything that requires forgiveness," Sarah said.

"You're only saying that because you were my partner in crime."

"The only crime I ever committed was with Zack—and you were at Bible study that night."

"Okay, maybe *misdeeds* is a more appropriate term," Claire amended.

"What misdeeds?" Sarah challenged.

"We skipped school. We smoked cigarettes. We drank alcohol. We snuck out to meet boys."

"In other words, we were normal teenagers."

"Yeah," Claire agreed. "But I'm Pastor Lamontagne's

daughter. I wasn't supposed to be a normal teenager. I was supposed to be better—or at least good. I definitely wasn't supposed to be found puking up vodka coolers under the bleachers after a football game or caught with my skirt up around my waist in Jacob Nolan's car."

"No one caught you with Jacob Nolan."

"They might as well have, because he told everyone who would listen that he popped the pastor's daughter's cherry in his cherry-red Firebird."

"Jacob Nolan was a jerk then and he's a jerk now," Sarah said. "But he was a mighty fine-looking jerk and yours wasn't the only cherry he popped in that car."

"No wonder I feel so special," Claire said dryly.

"My point is, your parents need to get over the so-called misdeeds of your teenage years and accept you for the wonderful person you are, and you need to stop doing penance for the same so-called misdeeds, give up on trying to earn their approval and let yourself be happy."

"I am happy."

"So you didn't go out and get a dog because you're lonely?"

"It is pretty quiet out here at night," she noted. "And maybe I was looking for something to keep me company—to sit under the desk when I'm working on the computer or snuggle up beside me on the sofa when I'm watching TV."

"Then Eduardo was a good choice," Sarah agreed. "Because I can't picture Devin under your desk—unless you were doing some creative role playing."

Claire rolled her eyes. "I told you that nothing is going to happen between me and Devin."

"I didn't believe you then and I don't believe you now."

And her friend was right to be skeptical, because having Ed around hadn't stopped her from thinking about Devin for more than five minutes.

She had yet to figure out what it was about the man that stirred her up inside. Aside from being outrageously handsome—a cross the entire Blake family had to bear—he wasn't anything like the men she was usually attracted to.

Or maybe her unexpected feelings for Devin were proof that she had finally learned from the mistakes of her past.

Except that she'd thought Eric was different, too.

And in the beginning, he had been. But eventually he'd turned out to be just like everyone else—wanting Claire to be somebody other than who she really was.

Chapter Eight

It took Ed almost a week to settle in at the ranch and accept that Claire was his new person. He seemed to enjoy hanging out at the stables with her, but he was smart enough to stay a safe distance away from most of the horses. He was still undecided about the goats. Sometimes he looked as if he wanted to join in with their prancing and playing, but he had yet to do so.

He did sometimes wander off to explore, and it pleased her to see him running across the fields, embracing the freedom of his new life. Thankfully, he never ventured too far and always came racing back when she called for him. He growled when visitors came to the ranch, and stuck close to Claire's side until he'd determined that the newcomers weren't a threat.

The following Thursday afternoon, Claire had just

finished grooming Jasmine when she heard Ed growling low in his throat.

"Do we have company?" she asked.

He stood at alert in the open doorway, his hackles up, his ears twitching.

She stepped out of Jasmine's stall to see what had snagged the dog's attention.

"It looks like we do have company," she said, her heart skipping a beat as she watched Devin climb out of his Range Rover.

He was in jeans and a T-shirt again today, with his cowboy boots on his feet.

It was the standard summer attire of half of the men in Haven—with a flannel shirt often donned over the T-shirt in the cooler months and a leather jacket added if it was really cold. In fact, she could walk down Main Street and, in only five minutes, cross paths with no less than a dozen men dressed exactly as Devin was dressed.

But seeing any of those other men had never made her heart race.

It wasn't fair that a tech geek should have such broad shoulders and strong arms. Of course, she knew that he was so much more than that, as he'd proven by the ease with which he'd controlled a twelve-hundred pound horse and his effortless hefting of hay bales. But he was as gentle as he was strong, as he'd demonstrated in his handling of the scared and wounded horses resident at Twilight Valley.

Devin Blake definitely wasn't "just" a computer nerd. He wasn't "just" anything. He was a complicated and complex man and the more she got to know him, the stronger her attraction to him grew.

I don't need a man. I've got plenty to keep me busy here on the ranch. And now I've got Ed, too.

And right now, the dog was practically vibrating with suppressed energy.

"It's okay, Ed. He's a friend."

But apparently the dog had already arrived at the same conclusion, because he gave a happy bark—a sound still rare enough to raise Claire's eyebrows—and raced across the yard to greet their visitor.

By the time she caught up to the dog, Devin was down on his haunches, using both hands to rub Ed's belly.

"Three days," she said, equal parts baffled and annoyed. "He was here for three days before he let me rub his belly."

Devin shrugged those mouthwateringly broad shoulders. "I told you animals like me."

She wasn't appeased by his easy explanation. "Is it because I'm female? Do you have something against women?"

"Not at all," Devin assured her.

She huffed out a breath. "I was talking to the dog."

"I figured." He grinned. "I was just clarifying my position."

Except his words hadn't clarified anything at all.

His actions over the past couple weeks didn't help, either.

Sometimes he was stiff and uncomfortable around her, but other times—like today—he came across as easygoing and even a little bit flirtatious. And he'd had the nerve to talk about *her* mixed signals.

Since she knew that she wasn't close to figuring out this man—and wasn't sure she wanted to—she focused on the dog instead.

"His previous owner was a woman," Claire said now. "Of course, so was her daughter, who took him to the shelter, so maybe he does have trust issues with women."

"You adopted him from the shelter," Devin said.

His remark sounded more like a statement than a question, but she nodded anyway. "I went with the hope of getting a puppy. There were six adorable beagle/Lab mix puppies—and then I saw Ed, looking so sad and helpless and alone."

"They teach them that look at the shelter, you know," Devin said. "So that visitors won't be able to resist taking them home."

"Well, I resisted," she told him.

"And yet I'm clearly looking at a dog that wasn't here the last time I was."

"I resisted for two whole days," she clarified.

He chuckled as he continued to rub the dog's belly. "If only someone had steered you toward the shelter five months ago, Ed could have been living in this paradise the whole time."

"Wait a minute—how did you know Ed was there five months?"

"I volunteer at the shelter."

She propped her hands on her hips. "So Ed didn't

run to you because animals like you," she realized. "He ran to you because he recognized you."

"*And* he likes me."

"What do you do at the shelter?"

"Mostly walk the dogs. They're allowed to run around in the dog park for an hour every day, but walking gives them additional exercise and leash training."

"Do you know another dog walker named David? One of the volunteers mentioned that she'd hoped he might adopt Ed."

Devin rolled his eyes. "Were you talking to Maureen?"

Claire nodded.

"When I first started volunteering at the shelter, Maureen could never remember my name, so she started calling me David. No matter how many times I told her it was Devin, she never got it right. So now I just answer to David—so much so that one of the new groomers actually thought my name was David."

She chuckled at that. "So how long have you been volunteering at the shelter?"

"A couple of years. My parents wanted me to find a hobby that would get me out of the house. Dad encouraged me to take up golfing, but I didn't really see the point in chasing a little white ball around a green field just to sink it into a cup."

"I've never understood golf, either," she confided. "But even worse than playing it is watching it on TV."

He shuddered. "You won't get any argument from me about that."

"So how did you go from not wanting to play golf to walking dogs?"

"My mom suggested that I get a pet," he told her. "So I went to the shelter and asked one of the managers what kind of dog she'd recommend for someone who works long and often erratic hours. After chatting some more about my lifestyle and work habits, Bonnie told me that she wouldn't even recommend a goldfish, because she wasn't sure I could be trusted to remember to feed it once a day.

"I thought she was kidding, but it turns out that shelter workers don't joke about things like that."

"Ouch," Claire said.

He nodded. "When I insisted that I wanted a dog, she suggested that I should spend some time at the shelter, so that I could see firsthand how much care and attention they needed. So I did—and I realized that she was right, that being responsible for a dog would require more time than I had to give.

"But I also realized that I was happy to spend a few hours at the shelter whenever I could. So now, when I've got some free time, I head over there, clip a leash onto a dog—or two or three—and take them out for some exercise and socialization."

"And now I feel guilty that the time you've been spending here and working on my website is taking you away from your dog walking."

"There's no need to feel guilty about anything," he said. "Getting away from my computer every once in a while is necessary to shake the cobwebs from my brain."

"Is that why you're here now?"

"Yeah. You mentioned that Hades doesn't get out a lot because most of your volunteers are afraid to ride him."

She nodded. "I was hoping to take him out this afternoon, but if you want to ride him, then Regina can get some exercise at the same time."

"Let's do it," Devin said.

Claire told herself she wasn't at all disappointed that he was only talking about taking a ride, but she wasn't entirely sure she believed it.

Devin hadn't given Claire a timeframe for the completion of her website, and she hadn't asked because she knew it was a side job for him and didn't expect him to take time away from his real work to do it. Yet since they'd first gone riding, he'd been back to the ranch so many times she'd lost count—not for anything to do with the website but to lend a hand with grooming or feeding the horses.

She might have thought that the visits were to spend time with her, except that they really didn't spend much time together. In fact, sometimes they were so busy with different tasks that they didn't exchange more than a few words. Other times, when they found themselves working in close proximity, the air fairly crackled with electricity.

And yet, the man still hadn't made a move, causing her to wonder if the attraction she felt was entirely one-sided.

Just when she'd convinced herself that it must be,

she'd caught him looking at her with unmistakable intensity before he'd quickly turned away, breaking the moment of connection.

So when Devin sent her a text message to tell her that he had some sample web pages for her to look at (finally!), she decided that maybe it was time to admit— to herself as much as him—that she'd changed her mind about not wanting to get involved.

Not that she was looking for a relationship, but she was no longer vehemently opposed to exploring the attraction that continued to simmer between them.

"Your message said that you had some mock-ups for me to look at," she reminded him.

"Uh…yeah. I do."

Devin was tripping over his thoughts and his words, flustered by her unexpected arrival at his door.

Again.

He hated being flustered, especially around Claire, though she didn't seem to mind when he stumbled trying to put a sentence together. She just waited patiently for him to gather his thoughts and translate them into something coherent.

"But I figured you'd text me back and we'd set up a time to talk and I'd show them to you on your computer," he said now.

"Except that they're not on my computer, they're on your computer," she pointed out.

"They would have been on yours, too, after you gave me remote access," he explained.

Her brow furrowed. "I don't know how to do that. I didn't even realize you *could* do that."

He smiled then, his discomfort abating as the conversation shifted closer to his area of expertise. "I would have walked you through it."

"Well, now you don't have to. Unless... Do you want me to go?" she asked.

"No," he answered quickly. "I mean, that wouldn't make a lot of sense, since you're already here."

Her lips curved. It wasn't the usual megawatt smile that stole the breath from his lungs, but a softer and somehow more intimate smile.

His heart knocked against his ribs. Hard.

"So you don't mind that I dropped by?"

"I don't mind," he said, surprised to realize it was true.

Because he was most often annoyed when people stopped by uninvited. But Claire wasn't people, she was...

Claire.

And for some reason, being around Claire made him happy.

Of course, being around Claire also made him think about things he shouldn't be thinking about—the scent of her hair, the softness of her skin and the shape of her lips—and want things he shouldn't be wanting—to slide his hands through those silky blond tresses, to caress every dip and curve of her body and taste the intoxicating flavor of her kiss.

Her smile widened then. "I know I should have called first, but I was in town to pick up a book from the library when I got your message, and since I had to drive right past here on my way back, I thought I'd take a chance that I'd catch you at home."

"I'm almost always home."

"I don't know about that," she said. "You've been spending a fair amount of time at Twilight Valley over the past few weeks. Often popping in with no advance warning."

Though the twinkle in her green eyes told him she was teasing, he realized it was true. And that his impromptu visits might sometimes be inconvenient for her.

It wasn't something he'd considered before, because whenever he headed out to the ranch, he'd only ever been thinking that he wanted to see her.

Not that he'd ever admit as much to her. Instead, he usually claimed that he was trying to reason through a technical glitch and that getting away from the problem for a couple of hours often helped him figure out the solution more easily when he got back to it. Which wasn't untrue, but it wasn't his real motivation, either.

"Is that a problem?" he asked now.

"No," she said. "I like having visitors. I like when *you* visit."

He swallowed. "You do?"

She nodded. "I enjoy talking to you. And I appreciate that you don't mind helping to muck out stalls while we're talking."

"Physical labor is sometimes a welcome change from sitting in front of monitors all day."

"I had a desk job for a few years," she confided.

"Did you hate it?"

"Only the sitting part. I liked most of the rest of it—

especially the people I worked with and the view from my office. Although, to be honest, I sometimes felt as if I was a kid playing at being grown-up, dressing up for my office job in clothes that I'd never wear around the ranch."

"You look plenty grown up to me," he told her.

"Do I?"

She'd tipped her head back to meet his gaze, and he was suddenly aware of how close they were standing. And that her mouth was only a few inches away from his.

"Yeah." He took a cautious step back, away from temptation. "Do you miss Austin?"

He caught a flicker of something in her eyes that might have been disappointment.

Or it might have been nothing at all.

"I miss the anonymity sometimes," she told him.

"Living in a small town can be like living in a fishbowl," he acknowledged.

And if they were actually living in a fishbowl, she'd be a butterfly betta and he'd be a glass catfish.

"But being part of a close-knit community has its benefits, too," he pointed out.

"You're right," she agreed. "Such as having a friend who has a cousin who builds websites."

He didn't bother to point out that building websites wasn't his job—it wasn't even a hobby—just something that he did on occasion if someone asked. Instead he said, "Why don't we go into my office to take a look at those mock-ups now?"

"Sounds good to me."

He led the way, then pulled out the chair behind his desk and gestured. "Sit."

She sat.

He stood beside her, so that he could control the mouse and click through the pages he'd set up. But when he glanced down, he realized that his vantage point afforded him a perfect view of the swell of her breasts above the low scoop neck of her T-shirt—and just a hint of peach-colored lace.

He swallowed hard and yanked his gaze to the trio of monitors.

"Oh, I like that," she said, when he'd displayed the first sample.

He'd taken one of the photos of the property that she'd provided and faded it out so that it was the background. The words *Twilight Valley Equine Rehabilitation and Retirement Facility* were centered at the top of the page in a bold, contemporary font, with *A Haven for Horses* in a smaller italicized version of the same typeface beneath it. Instead of a feature image, he'd opted for a slider that showcased additional photos of the property and some of its residents—including Lily and Daisy.

"I like that one, too," she said, when he showed her the second sample, essentially the same as the first, with a vertical navigation bar on the side of the page rather than a horizontal one beneath the header.

He chuckled softly.

She turned her head to look at him over her shoulder, and his breath caught as he inhaled the sweet scent of peaches. Her shampoo, he guessed. Or maybe a lotion that she rubbed on her skin.

His body stirred, and he gritted his teeth and shoved that mental image to the back of his mind for later consideration.

Much later.

She tipped her chin up, just a fraction, but suddenly her lips—glossy and pink—were mere inches from his again, and he was *oh-so-tempted* to lean forward and breach the scant distance that separated his mouth from hers.

Instead, he took a hasty step back, colliding with the cabinet that held his printers. The back of his thigh rapped against the sharp edge, making him swear ripely as his muscle immediately tightened in protest of the assault.

"Ohmygoodness." Claire pushed the chair away from the desk and dropped to her knees in front of him, her eyes level with his crotch.

Ohmygoodness, indeed.

"Are you okay?" She rubbed to loosen the tension in his hamstring muscle.

He definitely wasn't okay, though he was no longer feeling the charley horse in his leg. He could only feel her hand on his thigh—and a tightening low in his belly.

He grasped wildly for something else—*anything else*—to focus on.

```
for (let index = start_value; index < end_value;
index += increment_value)
```

"Devin?" she prompted.

"Fine." It was all he could manage through gritted teeth as he attempted to ease back again.

Slowly. Carefully.

```
for (let index = start_value; index < end_value;
index += increment_value)
```

But the cabinet was still there.

Claire's hand dropped away but she remained on her knees, and there was no way she could miss the fact that he was aroused.

Desperately and painfully aroused.

Chapter Nine

"Oh." Claire's gaze lifted to his then, her cheeks flushing prettily. "Um."

"Don't say anything else," Devin pleaded.

She gave a quick, jerky nod of assent.

"Just give me a minute to walk off this charley horse," he said.

She nodded again, and he quickly made his escape.

```
for (let index = start_value; index < end_value;
index += increment_value)
```

He paced the length of the main floor, from the living room to the kitchen and back again, reciting the simple code in an effort to *not* think about how he'd felt when Claire touched him.

When he was fairly confident that he was in control again—though certain he was going to have one heck of a bruise on his thigh tomorrow—he returned to the office.

Claire was standing by the wall of bookcases now, but she turned to face him when he entered the room.

"I was being nosey," she confided. "You certainly have a lot of toys."

"Collectibles," he said. And if she thought the few scattered around his office were *a lot*, he wondered what she'd think if she saw the room upstairs.

"And the difference between toys and collectibles is…price, I'm guessing?"

"Collectibles are an investment," he said.

"So…future price," she said, sounding amused.

"Plus, those are mint-in-box." Heat climbed up his throat.

"Mint-in-box." She smiled. "You really are one of those guys, aren't you?"

"Those guys?" he asked quizzically.

"Like Sheldon and Leonard," she clarified.

She was talking about *The Big Bang Theory* again.

"Have you ever been to Comic-Con?"

"Which one?"

Her smile widened. "I bet you've got a comic book collection, too."

"Upstairs," he said. Because apparently he did not know when to shut up.

"Well, you've got some interesting stuff here, but what really caught my eye was this." She picked up a simple walnut frame and turned it around so that he could see the image. It was a photo of him as a child, seated on the back of a horse. "You can't be more than, what—about four years old in this picture?"

"It's a pony," he said. "And I was three."

"Is that your grandfather holding the reins?"

He nodded. "Gramps put each of his grandkids in a saddle for the first time."

She tapped the photo. "Was this your first time?"

He nodded again.

"No wonder you looked so comfortable on horseback at the ranch," she mused, placing the photograph back on the shelf. "You were obviously a natural from the beginning."

"More likely I was just determined to prove I could do everything Trevor could do," he confided. "And I'd been watching him ride for two years already by then."

"I've got older brothers, too," she reminded him, sympathy in her tone. "But often when I was left behind, it wasn't only because I was younger but also because I was a girl."

"Who taught you to ride?" he asked her now.

"My uncle Mick. I was ten—and determined." She smiled at the memory. "Trying to keep up with Joss and Dee, his daughters, who'd been riding since they were about the same age as you in that picture."

"And did you?" he asked, though he was certain he already knew the answer.

"I didn't keep up. I made them eat my dust."

He chuckled.

She moved on from the picture to trail a fingertip over the spines of a series of books on the shelf. "Do you ever read for pleasure? Aside from the comic books upstairs, I mean."

"That *is* my pleasure reading shelf," he deadpanned.

"You read *Refactoring: Improving the Design of Existing Code* for fun?" she asked dubiously.

"It's a classic." Then he smiled, to let her know he was joking. "Actually, I have a Kindle loaded with an eclectic collection of popular fiction, nonfiction, biographies, histories and even some philosophy."

"I read *Meditations* by Marcus Aurelius in college—that's about the extent of my philosophical background," she confessed.

"It's a good start."

"Generally I prefer mysteries and thrillers, like Quinn Ellison writes," she told him.

"Have you read *The Attic*?" he asked, naming the author's latest title.

"That's what I was picking up at the library today."

"I preordered it for my Kindle, so I was able to start reading it on the release day—and finished it that night."

She wrinkled her nose. "You're one of those, are you?"

"One of those *what*?" he asked.

"A binge reader."

"You say that as if it's a bad thing."

She shrugged. "I just figure that it took the author a fair amount of time to write the story, so I should return the favor by savoring every word."

"I'm not sure the author cares how long it takes someone to read a book so long as it's read," he argued. "Plus, I don't want to have to worry that I'm going to hear any spoilers at The Daily Grind when I go in to grab a coffee the next day."

"Is there a book club that meets at the local coffee shop to discuss new releases?"

"Only Quinn's, because she's a local celebrity," he said.

Claire's jaw dropped. "She lives in Haven?"

"Cooper's Corners," he clarified.

"How did I not know this?"

He shrugged. "You just moved back to town a few months ago."

"I can't believe no one told me," she said, sounding disgruntled.

"I just did."

She huffed out a breath. "I meant *before now*."

"You're a fangirl," he realized.

"Maybe. A little."

Devin chuckled, starting to feel more at ease again.

Of course, the feeling didn't last long, because the next words out of Claire's mouth were: "Can I apologize for getting up close and personal?"

"I'd rather just forget about it," he told her, wondering that he didn't suffer whiplash from the abrupt change of direction of the conversation.

"What if I don't want to forget it?" she asked, sounding just a little bit hesitant.

"What?"

Claire tucked her hands into the front pockets of her jeans, striking a deliberately nonchalant pose. "I realize your…response…might have been a purely involuntary reaction to external stimuli," she said. "But

I was hoping it might be a sign that you're as attracted to me as I am to you."

He swallowed. "You're attracted...to me?"

"That shouldn't surprise you, considering that you overheard me refer to you as *a hottie* at our second meeting."

"Maybe not," he allowed. "But you're..."

She lifted a brow. "I'm...what?"

"Way out of my league," he concluded.

"Why do you think so?"

"Because—" He swallowed again. "Because you're friendly and personable and so incredibly beautiful."

"I'm flattered," she said. "And a little confused as to why you'd think any of that puts me out of your league."

"Because. I'm an awkward, introverted—and some people would even say antisocial—computer nerd."

"Maybe," she allowed. "But you're also really sweet and incredibly sexy."

He had no idea how to respond to that. How she wanted him to respond. So he cleared his throat and retreated to his comfort zone.

"We should, um, get back to the computer."

"It's interesting that this conversation is making you uncomfortable," she mused.

"I don't find that interesting at all."

She gave him a long, speculative look. "It is, because it wasn't that long ago that you were trying to get me to admit that I thought you were a hottie."

"I shouldn't have teased you about that," he acknowledged now.

"You're a regular Dr. Jekyll and Mr. Hyde, aren't you?"

"Nope. Just me."

"And you don't like people stopping by uninvited, do you?"

He wasn't comfortable with her scrutiny—and even less so with her insightful observations.

"I'm not good with…unplanned…social interactions," he admitted.

"I don't understand."

Of course she didn't.

No one did.

His family—and even his friends—made allowances for his "quirky personality," but they didn't really get it.

However, Claire was looking at him as if she wanted to understand, and he found himself wanting to explain it to her.

"My brain seems to function in two distinct modes," he confided. "Work mode is easy. When I'm in front of a computer, I'm dealing with numbers and problems and solutions."

"That's the easy part?" she asked dubiously.

"For me it is. It's social mode that I sometimes struggle with."

"Why only sometimes?"

"Maybe a train would be a better analogy," he decided. "It's as if my brain runs on two different tracks—the work track and the social track. The work track is where I chug along most of the time, but every once in a while—if I have a meeting at the office or need to make a quick trip to the grocery store—I consciously switch over to the social track, and then I can generally muddle through okay." He managed a smile then. "Some people even find me charming."

"But when you're unexpectedly put in a social situation without having had the opportunity to switch tracks—such as when someone shows up at your door without any warning—you find your wheels slipping on the rails," she guessed.

He nodded.

"I'm sorry," she said, sounding sincerely contrite.

"It's not your fault," he told her.

"Switching back to the work track," she said, obviously taking pity on him and his social ineptitude. "The second layout is my favorite."

"Why don't we look at the rest of them before you decide?"

"I did look at them. While you were walking off your...charley horse."

He felt heat creep up his throat again. "I guess it took a while to loosen the muscle."

And to restore the blood flow to his brain.

"I didn't think you'd mind if I scrolled through the designs on my own."

"I don't. Mind, I mean." He cleared his throat. "And you like the second one best?"

She nodded.

"But I think I prefer the font of the fifth one and the color scheme of the third one."

She was standing so close that he could smell the scent of her shampoo, and he couldn't seem to focus on anything else.

She smiled, as if she knew his mind had gone blank. "I wrote it all down for you on a Post-it."

"Okay."

"And now I should get back to the ranch," she said. "Ed doesn't like it when I'm gone too long."

"You should bring him with you next time," he said.

She smiled. "Next time I will. And I'll call first."

He smiled, too, because *next time* meant that he'd be seeing her again.

But, of course, he would—because he was building her website.

And she'd only stopped by today to check out his progress.

But even if that was true, they'd talked about other topics, too. Riding and reading and...

I was hoping it might be a sign that you're as attracted to me as I am to you.

The words echoed in his mind long after she'd gone.

And though he had work that needed to be done—including on the website for Twilight Valley—the realization that Claire Lamontagne was attracted to him had caused his train of thought to go completely off the rails.

I didn't see you at church this morning.

Claire winced at the text message from her mom, and again when she checked the time stamp and realized it had been sent several hours earlier.

Though it seemed like a simple and straightforward message, the words were weighted with disappointment and disapproval.

It was her own fault, Claire knew. Not only because she'd given them so much cause for disappointment and disapproval in the past, but also because she'd been attending Sunday services fairly regularly since her return to Haven. It was her way of offering the proverbial olive branch—a gesture of apology and repentance.

And though she didn't sit up front with her mom—she wasn't sure either of them was ready to take things that far—she went to church and she listened to her dad preach, and in doing so gave both her parents a little bit of hope that perhaps her soul wasn't completely unredeemable.

She was tempted to text a reply, but decided that her apologies would likely be better received in person.

So she cleaned up and drove into town, stopping at Sweet Caroline's to pick up a few treats on her way to the simple bungalow that had been her childhood home. Though her mother might express disapproval of decadent indulgences, she wouldn't let them go to waste.

"Hello, Claire."

She started at the sound of her father's voice as she walked past the doorway of his study. She hadn't expected him to be home. Sunday afternoons he was usually in his office at the church, where members of his congregation could seek him out for counsel or prayer.

"Hi, Dad." She dutifully went to him, sitting behind the big desk, and kissed his cheek. "Is everything okay at church?"

"Everything's fine," he assured her. "We've got a young pastor visiting from Oklahoma who's covering the office today."

"That must be a nice break for you. I mean, I know your work is a pleasure, not a burden, but—"

"But yes," he interrupted her rambling to agree. "It is a nice break. And though your mom didn't mention that you were stopping by, it's even nicer to see you here."

"Mom didn't know," Claire admitted.

"Well, it's good to have you home."

"It's good to be home," she said, no longer surprised to realize it was true.

"So—what's in the box?"

The eager tone of his question made her smile.

She broke the seal and opened the lid, letting him take his pick of the doughnuts.

"She'll be upset if this spoils my dinner," he warned, just before he bit into the sweet doughy goodness of the apple fritter he'd chosen.

"So don't let it spoil your dinner," Claire advised.

He was chuckling when she walked out of the room.

"Claire." Elsa carefully marked her page in the Bible and set it on the table beside her chair. "I didn't know you were going to stop by."

"I'll be sure to call first next time," she promised, touching her lips to her mother's cheek as she'd done with her father's.

"Did you want tea?" Elsa was already rising.

"Tea would be nice." She followed her mom into the kitchen.

"When you didn't reply to my text message, I thought maybe I'd overstepped."

"You didn't overstep," she said, wondering if she and her mother would ever have a relationship where they didn't feel the need to tiptoe around one another. "And I'm sorry I missed church this morning. I was just so exhausted when I fell into bed last night that I completely forgot to set my alarm."

"Ranching is hard work," Elsa observed. "And hardly suitable work for a young woman on her own."

"I'm taking care of horses, not herding cattle, Mom."

"I know what you're doing, and I worry about you."

"Well, you can worry less now," she said brightly. "Because I've got Ed to keep an eye out for me."

Her mother sucked in a breath. "You stopped by to tell us that you've shacked up with another man."

Apparently, the tiptoeing was over.

"Ed isn't a man," Claire said, ignoring the hurt she felt at her mother's sharp words. "He's a dog."

Her mom's mouth snapped shut and she poured the boiling water into the teapot.

"You might have led with that," she said.

An admonishment rather than an apology.

Not that Claire had expected one.

"Obviously I should have," she agreed.

"So you got a dog," Elsa said.

"A shepherd/collie mix, about five years old."

"A rescue." Her mom smiled at that. "I should have figured."

"Anyway, Ed's the reason I forgot to set my alarm," Claire said. "He had a run-in with a skunk last night and I had to scrub him with a mixture of hydrogen peroxide, baking soda and dish soap. We went through the routine five times before I got enough of the stink off of him to let him in the house."

"Poor thing," Elsa murmured.

"Are you talking about me or the dog?"

"I was talking about the dog," her mom said. "But I imagine it was quite the ordeal for you, too."

"It was," she agreed. "But I don't think Ed will be chasing after more skunks any time soon."

"I ran into Maris Prescott at The Trading Post yesterday," Elsa said, shifting the topic of conversation again. "I'm sure you remember her from high school."

"I do," she said. As if she'd ever forget the girl who'd told everyone in their eleventh grade math class that Claire had given blow jobs to half the football team. It wasn't true, of course, but no one was willing to take the word of someone who'd lost her virginity to Jacob Nolan over that of the founder of the Chastity Club. "Though she was Maris Green back then."

"And green-eyed with jealousy," Sarah had remarked. "The only reason she started that stupid club is that none of the boys want to have anything to do with her."

That memory almost made Claire smile.

"Well, she asked about you," her mom continued. "And commented that it's a wonderful and worthwhile thing you're doing at Twilight Valley."

"Did you tell her that you disagreed?"

"I don't disagree," Elsa told her. "I never said that your work wasn't worthwhile—I just don't think it's work that you should be doing."

And since they'd pretty much come full circle, Claire decided it was a good time to go.

"Whether I should or shouldn't, there is work to be done and I need to get back to it."

She kissed her mom goodbye and headed back to the ranch, wondering why she continued to let herself hope for a better relationship with her parents when that hope seemed destined to remain unfulfilled.

Chapter Ten

Crescent Moon stood close by, watching as Claire groomed the most recent addition to the stable. Mystic was a six-year-old gelding that his previous owner had tried to train in the art of dressage. Unfortunately his primary method of training involved a heavy hand and a crop.

"I haven't forgotten you," she promised her long-time equine companion. "But you've always been loved and taken care of, and this poor fella hasn't lived such a charmed life."

Of course, that was an understatement, she acknowledged, as she gently worked on the trembling gelding.

"He's going to need a lot of time and attention."

Because when it became evident that beating the horse didn't garner the desired results, Mystic had essentially been abandoned to his own devices.

"But eventually, hopefully, Mystic's going to realize that this is a place of healing."

Certainly Twilight Valley had proven to be that for Claire.

"I thought you'd stop talking to your horses once you got a dog."

Claire glanced over her shoulder to see that Devin was holding up his phone, snapping pictures of her with the horse.

He'd texted to let her know that he would be coming out to the ranch to take some more photos for the website, and obviously he wasn't wasting any time.

"Ed's off chasing squirrels or rabbits or whatever else he can find."

"A ranch like this must be paradise to a dog—especially one who spent the last five months in a shelter."

"He seems happy here," she agreed.

He frowned as he scrolled through the pictures he'd taken.

"Problem?" she asked. "We can move to a paddock on the other side of the barn if you think the lighting would be better there."

"It's not the lighting," he said. "It's that you look like May, and I'm not sure that's the look we're going for."

"Who's May?" she wondered aloud.

"I mean the month of May—in a sexy cowgirl calendar."

Her lips curved. "You think I'm sexy?"

He cleared his throat. "It's, um, not really an opinion but a fact."

"Or maybe it's your opinion that it's a fact."

He kept his gaze purposely fixed on the screen of his phone.

Claire knew she shouldn't tease him, but he was just so darn cute when he was flustered that she couldn't seem to help herself.

"Okay, what do I need to do to not look like May?"

"Untie your shirt."

Her brows lifted. "Are you asking me to take off my top?"

"No!"

His response was so vehement, she had to laugh. "Maybe you should clarify what you want, Devin."

He swallowed. "I want—I mean, for the pictures, I don't think you should be showing so much...skin."

She followed his gaze to her bare midriff.

It was an unseasonably warm day, so she'd untucked her shirt and tied the tails into a knot below her breasts, exposing several inches of skin above the low waist of her jeans.

She didn't think there was anything particularly risqué about the look, but the focus of the website was supposed to be the horses and she didn't want to take any attention away from them. So she tucked the comb into her back pocket and began to unknot the front of her shirt. Watching Devin as he watched her, as if she was performing some sort of reverse striptease.

When her midriff was once again covered—and she was certain that had been just a flash of disappointment in his eyes as she tucked the tails of the shirt into her jeans—she returned to her grooming and Devin resumed his picture taking.

When she was finished with the gelding, she gave him an apple and a gentle kiss on the nose.

"He's made a lot of progress in a short period of time," Devin noted.

"He has," she concurred. "For some animals, removing them from the source of the trauma is enough to start them on the road to recovery. For others, especially those who have suffered abuse at the hands of different people and in different places, it's a much more arduous journey."

"You'll send me his bio, to be included on the site?" he asked.

"Of course," she agreed. "Now I've got a question for you."

"Okay," he said again.

She breached the distance between them, then tipped her head back to meet his gaze. "Have you thought about kissing me?"

His Adam's apple bobbed as he swallowed. "You don't believe in being subtle, do you?"

"I've tried being subtle. And maybe I was too subtle, because you didn't pick up on any of my cues."

"You know I'm better with computers than people," he said. "Whenever there's room for interpretation, I tend to misinterpret."

"Which is why I decided to abandon subtlety," she told him.

"I guess that's fair."

"Now…are you going to answer my question?"

"Yes," he finally said.

"Yes, you're going to answer my question? Or yes, you've thought about kissing me?"

His gaze shifted to her lips, lingered there. "Yes, I've thought about kissing you."

A slow, liquid warmth spread through her body, heating her from head to toe and everywhere in-between.

"Are you ever going to move beyond thinking to actually doing?" she asked.

"There's a lot to think about," he said. "Starting with the fact that your best friend is my cousin."

"While you're thinking about that, I'm going to do this," she said, lifting her arms to link her hands behind his head and draw his mouth down to hers.

Claire's mother had often warned that her impulsive behavior was going to get her into trouble someday. Of course, Elsa Lamontagne had ominous warnings about everything, and her daughter had rarely heeded any of them.

And if her decision to make the first move rather than waiting for Devin to do so was impulsive, she wasn't regretting it now. Because even if he wasn't very adept at picking up a woman's cues, he certainly knew what to do when it came to taking action.

Yes, she'd initiated the contact, but Devin quickly—and expertly—took over. For a man who obviously prided himself on his higher-level thinking skills, he had some serious talent in the kissing department. So much so that her knees actually went weak, and she realized it was a good thing he was holding her close, or she might have slid to the ground.

On the other hand, the ground beneath their feet was spread with fresh bedding, and the idea of a literal roll in the hay with Devin gave her a quick thrill.

It had been more than ten months since she'd been with a man. More than ten months since she'd experienced the pleasure of touching and being touched. For most of that time, she hadn't thought about what she was missing.

But she was thinking about it now.

His tongue touched hers, and heat sparked through her veins, electrifying her every nerve ending. His hands skimmed up her back, and she actually trembled, the intensity of her own desire for this man shaking her to the core, obliterating her ability to think.

And she needed to think.

No more men. No more heartbreak.

Unfortunately, the reminder came a little too late this time.

Because now that she was in Devin's arms, her fingers digging into the hard muscles of his broad shoulders, her breasts pressing against the solid wall of his chest, her lips tingling from his kiss, she was reminded of all the good stuff that came before the heartbreak.

Like man-made orgasms.

Yet somehow, she managed to push that tempting thought aside and end the kiss.

"Apparently you have many talents," she noted, lifting a hand to touch her still tingling lips.

"Same goes," he said.

She was gratified to note that he was every bit as breathless as she was.

And while the ground was starting to feel a little steadier beneath her feet, her heart was still thundering like Crescent Moon's hooves in a full-out gallop.

She took a minute to draw air into her lungs and attempt to slow her racing pulse before she asked, "Are you still thinking?"

"Only about how much I want to kiss you again."

She wanted that, too. And a lot more.

But she didn't want to rush into anything.

Not this time.

Not with Devin.

"I think we might need to ration those kisses—they're pretty potent," she cautioned.

"I think you're right. And I should get home to see how I can use these pictures," he said.

"Okay," she agreed, torn between relief and disappointment that he was once again deferring to her wishes.

"I do have one question, though, before I go."

"Okay," she said again.

"Have you changed your mind about not wanting to get involved?"

"It's a pretty big leap from a single kiss to a personal involvement, don't you think?"

"Is it?" he wondered.

A fair question, considering the potency of the single kiss they'd just shared.

"Let's say that I'm no longer opposed to seeing where things might go," she told him.

He nodded, apparently satisfied by her response.

Meanwhile, Claire was feeling distinctly *un*satisfied.

But taking a step back was smart.

And she needed to be smart.

"I should have the website done by the weekend. Of course, I'll let you take a look at it and give your final approval before it goes live."

"So I'll probably see you sometime on the weekend?" she asked hopefully.

"Or maybe sooner."

"If you wanted to stop by tomorrow afternoon, my newest resident—a retired Derby champion from Palo Alto—should be here." Because she didn't want to wait even a few days to see him again.

"Don't most owners breed their champions rather than put them out to pasture?"

"They do," she confirmed. "But Regent's Rebel is sterile. In other words—worthless."

"But not to you."

"He's a beautiful horse with a lot of life and spirit in him yet," she noted. "He's not winning races anymore, but he still loves to run."

"Will you keep him here or rehome him?"

"I'd love to keep him. I'd love to keep them all," she admitted. "But since I can't, I'll do what I can to find a suitable stable for him to live out his final years."

"I'll swing by tomorrow to meet him," Devin decided. "And maybe take Hades out for a run."

"I appreciate the help," she said. "And…and I like having you around."

"That's good," he said. "Because I like being here."

She was smiling as she walked with him to his vehicle, Ed—having returned from his adventures—trotting along at their heels.

Devin wasn't entirely sure how he managed to make it home without crashing his SUV, because his mind sure as hell hadn't been on his driving. Even now, as he walked through his town house and settled himself in front of his computer, he wasn't thinking about what he was supposed to be doing. Instead, he was thinking about Claire.

More specifically, he was thinking about kissing Claire.

Or maybe marveling over the fact that he'd been kissing Claire.

There were very few people that he was comfortable with, but he was comfortable with her. Despite his hyperawareness of the attraction that sizzled between them, she had a way of making him feel at ease in her company, accepted for who he was.

He'd thought they were becoming friends.

He thrilled to the idea that they could be more.

Because while it still boggled his mind that she actually seemed to *like* him, it was apparent that she did.

And just thinking about that kiss, about holding Claire in his arms, was enough to make him hard again.

How long had it been since he'd felt the press of a woman's soft curves against him?

Too damn long.

And though he'd barely said goodbye to her thirty minutes earlier, he already couldn't wait to see her again.

* * *

Thursday afternoon, after Claire had finished her chores—including placing an order at the feed store—she looked at Ed, lounging in the grass, looking bored.

Or maybe he was just relaxed.

It was hard to tell with Ed sometimes.

But she knew that he enjoyed watching the scenery pass by the window when he accompanied her into town, so she said, "You want to go for a ride?"

The magic words made the dog's tail wag, and Claire laughed, pleased to see such an immediate and obvious sign of enthusiasm. Happy to know that he was happy.

It had been exactly two weeks since she'd brought him home, and he was settling in nicely. He still slept with the pink unicorn, but he played with some of the other toys she'd bought him and even slept on his new doggy bed in the corner of her bedroom—except when it stormed.

Thunder, she'd recently discovered, turned her usually brave dog into a great big fraidy cat.

"Well, come on then." She jingled her keys and he raced to the truck.

As soon as she opened the door, Ed hopped into the cab and scooted across the bench seat to the passenger side to press his nose against the window.

"It would be nice if you waited for me to roll down the window before you tried to shove your head out of it," she grumbled. "It's not an easy task to wipe doggy nose prints off the glass."

Ed stayed where he was, with his nose stuck to the glass.

With a sigh of resignation, she started the engine, then lowered the window a few inches so that he could get some air.

"Maybe we'll order pizza from Jo's for dinner tonight," she said, thinking aloud as she turned onto the highway toward town.

Ed turned to look at her then with a hopeful expression on his face.

"Sorry—I shouldn't have said *we*, because there's no way I'm going to share my cheese and sausage pizza with a lactose intolerant dog."

He offered a plaintive whine of protest.

"I swear, half the time you know exactly what I'm saying," she mused. "The other half of the time you only pretend that you don't have a clue."

But at least he listened.

And he usually stuck pretty close to her side, providing her with the companionship she'd been seeking when she visited the animal shelter.

"You're everything I was looking for—everything I need," she said, perhaps attempting to convince herself more than the dog.

And maybe it was true, but since the kiss that she'd shared with Devin two days earlier, she couldn't deny that she wanted more.

More kisses.

More Devin.

And maybe she could enjoy more of both if she invited him out to the ranch to share her pizza.

Ed waited in the truck while she went inside the feed store to pay for her purchases and Bryan Rockell loaded them into the back of her truck, sending her off with a wave and a wink that she knew was meant to remind her that he'd seen her naked—even if that forgettable event had taken place nearly a decade earlier.

Eager to make her escape, lest he think she was hanging around to chat or flirt with him, Claire drove out of the parking lot and around the corner before pulling over to call Jo's and place her order.

"We've got half an hour to kill before the pizza will be ready. Do you think that's a good excuse to stop by Devin's house?"

Ed, clearly recognizing the name, responded with a happy bark.

"He might not be happy to see us," she warned, as she pulled away from the curb and continued along Station Street.

And maybe she hoped that he wouldn't be, because a grumpy Devin had to be a lot less appealing than the one who'd kissed her senseless in the barn.

"He doesn't like to be interrupted when he's working—and I know he's working on finishing my website—but we won't stay long."

Just long enough to ensure that he'd be thinking about her when she left—and maybe long enough for another one of those bone-melting kisses.

Because she was fantasizing about the kiss, it took her a moment to realize that Ed's enthusiasm for their outing had noticeably waned. And when she turned onto Porter Road, taking the back route to Devin's neighborhood to avoid the heavier traffic on Main Street, he drew his head back into the cab and hunkered down in his seat.

"What's the matter, buddy?"

Not that she actually expected a response, but she hoped for some kind of reaction—a sideways glance or a twitch of his ears.

He gave her nothing.

She reached over to scratch behind his ears. After his unicorn, belly rubs and sweet potato doggy treats, he liked ear scratches best.

Still no response.

Not even a half-hearted wag of his tail.

"Now you're scaring me, Ed."

She pulled into Devin's drive and shifted into Park, then turned her full attention to the dog.

"Are you sick?"

He hadn't appeared to be feeling unwell when they'd left the ranch, but there was definitely something wrong with him now.

"Hold tight, buddy. I'll be right back," she promised.

As soon as Devin opened the door, the frantic worry that she'd been trying to hold at bay suddenly overwhelmed her and her eyes filled with tears.

"What's wrong?" he asked, immediately concerned. "Are you hurt?"

She shook her head. "It's Ed."

"Is he sick?"

"I don't know what's wrong. I have to take him to the vet. I should have gone directly there when I realized he was acting weird, but we were already on our way here."

"Give me your keys," Devin said. "I'll drive."

Claire didn't protest being told what to do.

She was too worried about Ed to be anything other than grateful that Devin was willing to take charge. She sat with one hand on the dog and her phone in the other, calling the veterinarian clinic.

Thankfully the clinic wasn't busy, and they were immediately led into an exam room to wait for Dr. Stafford when they arrived.

Of course Devin knew Brooke Stafford because she was married to his cousin, and Claire had become well acquainted with the vet during her visits to Twilight Valley, but when the doctor walked into the room, it was Ed that she greeted first.

"I've known him since he was a puppy," Brooke explained. "And I did his wellness check at the shelter before they made him available for adoption. I assume that's where you got him?"

Claire nodded. "I've only had him a couple weeks, but I've never seen him like this."

"I'll give him a quick exam while you tell me about the events of his day to see if we can't pinpoint what's wrong with him."

While Claire summarized their morning routine and trip into town, Brooke listened to Ed's heart and lungs; palpitated his torso to check his lymph nodes, internal organs and legs; examined his eyes, ears and teeth and observed him walking, standing and sitting.

The dog submitted to the doctor's poking and prodding without protest. Without any reaction at all, in fact.

After exchanging a brief greeting with the vet, Devin had been quiet, but he stood close behind Claire, a hand on her back, offering silent support.

When Brooke finished looking over the dog, she made some notes on his chart.

"What's wrong with him?" Claire asked worriedly.

"Absolutely nothing that taking him home won't cure," the vet promised.

"I don't understand."

"Ed has always been an incredibly sensitive animal," Brooke told her. "Even when he was a puppy, Joyce reported that changes to his routine would put him out of sorts.

"And you've only had him a couple weeks, so he probably doesn't yet feel completely settled with you, and when you drove from the feed store to Devin's house today, your route took you past the animal shelter."

And suddenly the dog's abrupt mood change made sense.

"He thought I was taking him back," Claire realized.

"That's my guess," Brooke agreed.

Claire's eyes filled with fresh tears. "Oh, Ed. You sweet, silly dog." She wrapped her arms around him, but only got a look of reproach in return. "I told you we were going to see Devin."

"But he'd never been to my house before," Devin pointed out. "Before you took him home to Twilight

Valley, most of the time he'd spent with me was at the shelter."

"I feel so foolish," Claire said now.

"You should never feel foolish for worrying about a pet. And while he should be fine when you get him home—" Brooke offered her a business card "—if you're still worried, give me a call. My cell phone number's on the back."

"Thank you."

"He's a good dog." The vet gave Ed a treat from the jar on the counter. "I'm glad to know that he's found another good home."

Chapter Eleven

Though Claire was still feeling a little shaky inside after the long drive back to Twilight Valley, she took her phone out of her pocket and pulled up Devin's contact information.

He answered on the first ring. "You're home?"

"We're home," she confirmed. "And Brooke was right. Ed's fine. In fact, right now, he's chasing Daisy and Lily. Well, he's on one side of the fence and they're on the other, but that seems to be what they do."

"How are *you*?" Devin asked her.

"Embarrassed."

"There's no reason to feel embarrassed. We were both worried about Ed."

But she was the only one who'd been crying when they rushed into the veterinarian clinic.

She was crying again now, but they were tears of relief this time and Devin couldn't see them.

"And I'm hungry," she admitted.

"Hungry?"

"I ordered pizza from Jo's for dinner, but then everything happened with Ed and I completely forgot about it."

"Do you want me to pick it up and bring it out to you?"

"I couldn't ask you to do that," she protested.

"You didn't ask—I offered."

"I could make something here," she said. And if she did so, she'd probably be eating before Devin could make the trip to the ranch. "But I really was craving pizza."

"I'll be there in half an hour."

He was true to his word.

Of course, the pizza had been sitting on the counter at Jo's for a while by the time he showed up, and then on the passenger seat of his SUV for another thirty minutes, so it was barely lukewarm by the time he delivered it.

"Jo said that ten minutes in a four-hundred-degree oven should heat it up nicely."

"Cold pizza is better than no pizza," she said. "And I'm too hungry to wait even ten more minutes. Unless you want it heated?"

"Oh." He was taken aback by the question. "I, um, wasn't planning on staying."

"Did you really think I'd let you pick up my pizza, deliver it to me and then send you away without sharing it?" She tugged him over the threshold, making it clear that she wanted him to stay.

"It's a large," he noted, following her into the house. "I thought maybe you were expecting company."

"I always order a large, so that I have leftovers," she told him.

"And if I stay, I'll deprive you of leftovers," he pointed out.

She turned to face him then. "Devin," she said patiently, "I would very much like you to stay and have dinner with me."

"Okay," he finally relented. Because he very much wanted to stay.

"Do you mind if we eat in the family room so we can watch the ball game?" Claire said. "The Astros are playing the A's."

Of course he didn't mind. But he was surprised. "You like baseball?"

"What's not to like?"

And with those words, Devin fell halfway in love with her—at least until he realized that she was cheering for the wrong team.

While they argued about the game and ate their pizza, Ed stuck close by, lying on the carpet in front of the TV chewing on an elk antler.

"I didn't mean to drag you away from your work—again," Claire said. "But I'm glad you're here."

"I don't mind being dragged away when you're the one doing the dragging," he said, and leaned in to brush his mouth over hers.

He didn't touch her anywhere else—their lips were

the only point of contact, but it was all that was required to hold her under his spell, captivated by the man as much as his kiss.

Desire heated her blood and spread through her veins, making her yearn. She curled her fingers around the edge of the sofa cushion, digging her nails into the soft fabric so that she wouldn't reach for him. Because she knew that if she touched him now, she wouldn't want to stop.

And while she'd pretty much decided that she was ready to take the next step, she wasn't sure that it was the right time for that step. Her emotions had been on enough of a roller coaster already today.

"Every bit as potent as I remembered," he said when he eased his lips from hers.

"It's only been two days," she pointed out.

"Actually, fifty-four hours and twenty-two minutes."

She laughed. "You just made that up. Didn't you?"

He grinned. "It's not precisely accurate, but I think it's a pretty good estimate off the top of my head."

Ed nosed his way between them.

"I think your dog's jealous," Devin said.

"I think you're right," she agreed. "But is he jealous of you? Or me?"

He chuckled. "Either way, I should probably go so that you can give him your undivided attention."

Claire smiled—until she realized that Ed's breath smelled like sausage. Then her gaze darted to the pizza box, noting that the lid—which she knew she'd closed—was open and the two slices that had been left were gone.

"Ed," she said, her voice stern.

He ducked his head.

"It's probably a good sign that the events of earlier today didn't affect his appetite," Devin said to Claire.

"But he ate two whole slices of pizza. That's a lot of cheese."

"I thought you were annoyed because he'd taken your leftovers. Why are you focused on the cheese?"

"Because he's lactose intolerant." She was already opening the windows.

"It can't be that bad," he said.

"Stick around for another ten minutes and then tell me it's not so bad."

She walked him out, and he kissed her again.

Ed followed them to the door and sat with his head tilted to one side, as if he was trying to understand this kissing thing.

Then he farted.

"When you come up for air after kissing a beautiful woman, that is not the air you want to be breathing," Devin said, waving his hand in front of his face, as if that might help the smell dissipate.

Ed stood at the door, whining.

Devin pushed it open and the dog took off, then Claire stepped out onto the porch with him. "I warned you."

"You did," he agreed.

"If you'd left ten minutes earlier, you could have avoided that whole episode."

His gaze dropped to her lips and his own curved in a slow, sexy smile that sent tingles through her veins.

"Totally worth it."

* * *

Sixteen hours and—Claire glanced at the time displayed on her fitness band—thirty-nine minutes after she'd watched Devin's SUV drive away from the ranch Thursday night, he was back again. She finished applying Bolt's hoof boot, pleased that the abscess she'd discovered earlier in the week was almost completely healed, then stripped off her gloves and tossed them in the garbage.

Devin climbed out of his vehicle and stopped to fuss over the dog, who'd rushed to greet him.

"Ed seems to have bounced back—from both the drive past the animal shelter and gorging on pizza," he remarked, when Claire made her way over to him.

"He has," she confirmed. "Though he's been pretty lazy this morning, no doubt still tired because his gas kept us both up last night."

"And how are you—besides tired?"

"Bored," she said. "My day has been completely uneventful."

"Maybe I can help with that."

Her brows lifted. "I'm listening."

"Why don't we go inside?"

If he'd been anyone else, she might have been wary. But this was Devin, who didn't seem to have a manipulative bone in his body.

"You finished my website?" she guessed.

He nodded. "Until you ask me to add more pages, anyway."

"I asked nicely," she reminded him, leading him toward the house and into the office on the main level.

She opened up her laptop and signed in—because Devin had insisted that she add at least that basic level of security to her computer after his first visit to the ranch—then he leaned over her shoulder and tapped away on the keyboard to open up the site.

Claire was quiet for a minute, scanning the page.

"This is...wow."

"Are you sure it's what you want? Because it's not too late to make changes."

"It's better than what I wanted," she said. "And I mean that sincerely. I had no idea that it would look this good."

There was so much to take in, she didn't know where to focus first. There was the header, the navigation bar, the slider—

"Oh." She paused the slideshow. "I haven't seen that picture before."

But she remembered when it was taken—the day he'd come out to the ranch when she was grooming Mystic. The day she'd kissed Devin.

But the photo was of her kissing Mystic—a reward for the horse's patience, and one he likely appreciated a lot less than the apple she'd also given him.

"I thought it was a pretty good shot—and a good depiction of what you're doing here, not just rescuing and respecting the horses in your care, but loving them."

"It's a great shot," she said, feeling inexplicably emotional that he'd managed to perfectly capture what she was doing at Twilight Valley not just with the image but his words.

She finished the slideshow, then perused the navigation bar. "What's this?"

She didn't wait for an answer but clicked on the link titled "Wish List" and discovered that it was, in fact, a wish list of everyday essentials, standard equipment and even big-ticket items.

"We didn't talk about this—I mean, we talked about it, but we didn't discuss putting it on the website."

"I know," Devin agreed. "And if you don't want to include it, I can take the page down. But for site visitors who don't want to commit to sponsoring a horse but want to do something more than toss a few dollars your way, this gives them an opportunity to make a tangible contribution, to buy a sack of grain or pay for a vet visit or direct their funds toward a bigger purchase."

"I definitely want to include it," she said. "Thank you."

"You're welcome."

"And now you can hit me with your bill—because whatever this is going to cost me, I'm convinced it's worth every penny."

"I'm not going to bill you for my work," Devin said.

"What are you talking about? Of course you have to bill me."

"Actually, I don't," he said.

"You suggested that you might offer a friends-and-family discount, but I never expected that to be one hundred percent."

"Consider it a donation of my services to Twilight Valley," he said.

"It's an incredibly generous one," she acknowledged.

He shrugged. "I'm happy to help."

"Seriously, I don't know how I can ever repay you for this."

"No repayment is necessary," he assured her.

"Then you need to add a footnote to the website, indicating that you created the website for Twilight Valley."

"No."

"Why not?" she asked, curious about his firm refusal.

"Because then I'd have other people wanting me to do their websites."

"Why would that be a problem?"

"Because I don't do websites," he told her.

"And yet," she pointed out.

"A favor for a friend."

"It was a big favor," she noted. "I might not know much—or anything—about website design, but even I can tell you put a lot of work into this."

"Well, if you really want to do something for me..." he ventured hesitantly. "You could...maybe...go out for dinner with me sometime."

And shy Devin was back, Claire realized. As if he worried that he might be crossing a line with his invitation.

"How would my going out for dinner with you be, in any way, a repayment for your work?" she wondered.

"Because I would get to enjoy the pleasure of your company."

"I've got a better idea," she said. "I'll cook for you."

"I wasn't angling for an invitation."

"I didn't think you were. And, as it happens, I like to cook."

"You do?"

"Mostly for other people," she admitted. "Cooking for one gets boring after a while."

"Tell me about it," he said. "I don't even have to look at the instructions on the Hungry-Man boxes anymore."

She laughed at that. "So tell me what kind of food you like."

"Food I don't have to cook."

"Okay…what kind of food don't you like?"

"Food I have to cook."

"I'm sensing a theme here."

"I'm sure I'd like whatever you made," he assured her. "But I'd really like to take you out… If you wanted to go out."

"Maybe next time," she said. "But tomorrow night, I'd like to make dinner for you."

Devin needed to get out of the house.

Claire had suggested six o'clock for dinner Saturday night and he'd been watching the clock since he woke up, as if that might somehow make the minutes tick by faster.

Desperate for a distraction, he headed to his brother and sister-in-law's house. Trevor wasn't home—having been sent out with the grocery list—but Devin didn't mind, because he enjoyed hanging out with Haylee and Aidan and Ellie just as much.

"I heard a rumor that my favorite niece and nephew are going to California for two weeks at the end of the summer," Devin remarked, as he bounced Aidan on his knee.

"They're your only niece and nephew." Haylee finished wiping Ellie's sticky hands, then unbuckled her daughter from the high chair and set her on the floor. "And you might not want to jostle them too much—they just ate."

Because of course she knew that Ellie would immediately crawl over to Devin so that he could bounce her on his other knee.

The twins were toddlers now, and though they were getting steadier on their feet every day, they still opted to move on all fours when they wanted to move fast.

"They're my only niece and nephew *so far*," he acknowledged, as he helped Ellie take position. "But maybe the belated honeymoon you're finally going to take will change that."

"If I thought there was the slightest possibility that might be true, I wouldn't be going," his sister-in-law said. "Two kids in diapers are enough."

"Of course, you probably didn't think there was the slightest possibility you'd end up pregnant with twins after spending one night with my brother," he remarked.

"I didn't," she confirmed. "But I was also so naive and inexperienced, I didn't realize that condoms had expiration dates."

"Are you saying…" Devin shook his head. "Sorry. It's none of my business."

"Your brother didn't tell you that I was a virgin before he and I slept together?" Haylee asked, clearly unconcerned about the boundaries of propriety.

"No." And why did his face suddenly feel so hot? "We don't usually share the intimate details of our relationships."

But for Devin, her revelation answered the one question that his brother had always refused to—why Trevor hadn't asked for a paternity test before stepping up to take responsibility for Haylee's pregnancy.

"Well, it really wasn't the big deal he made it out to be. Or maybe it was a bigger deal than I wanted to admit," she allowed.

"He didn't know?"

She shook her head. "I was afraid that, if he knew, he'd change his mind about wanting to be with me," she confided. "Men can be weird about the innocence thing."

"You think so?"

"I know so—the way he reacted afterward was proof enough."

Devin stopped bouncing his knees and stretched out his legs so the twins could dismount. They immediately started climbing him like a jungle gym.

"Do you think a woman would freak out to discover a man that she slept with had less experience than she did?"

"Hmm." Haylee continued to tidy the kitchen as she considered the question. "I guess I'm wondering how she'd find out—because a man's lack of experience isn't as obvious, is it?"

"Isn't it?" he asked. "I mean, wouldn't it be apparent that he lacked...finesse?"

"You're asking the wrong woman," she said with a

laugh, joining him in the family room adjacent to the kitchen and sitting down beside him on the carpet.

Aidan immediately abandoned his uncle to climb into his mother's lap and rub his cheek against her shoulder. "Ready for a nap now, are you?"

The little boy shook his head, but his thumb popped into his mouth and his eyes began to close.

Ellie, meanwhile, showed no signs of slowing down.

"So tell me about her," Haylee said, as she rubbed circles on her son's back.

"Who?"

"This more experienced woman you're seeing."

"I don't know that I'm really seeing her. I mean, I see her, obviously. But we've never been out on a date or anything like that."

"Why not?"

"Maybe because I haven't actually asked," he realized. "Well, I did suggest that we should go out for dinner sometime, but then she offered to make dinner instead."

"Is this Sarah's friend?" she guessed. "The one you're doing the website for?"

He frowned. "How do you know that?"

"Trevor mentioned it."

"He did?"

She nodded. "He pays more attention than you obviously give him credit for."

"And apparently has no secrets from his wife," Devin remarked dryly.

"Was it supposed to be a secret?"

"No," he admitted. "I mean, it wasn't supposed to be

anything more than a business association. She needed a website and I know how to build a website."

"But you like her."

"Yeah."

"And she obviously likes you."

He thought about the kisses they'd shared—and was punished for his daydreaming by a sock-clad foot to his cheek as Ellie tried to climb over his shoulder.

He snagged the back of her shorts and lifted her off his back, making her giggle.

"Yeah," he said again, in response to his sister-in-law's question.

"So when are we going to meet her?"

"I just told you that we haven't even been on an actual date—there's no way I'm going to freak her out by offering to introduce her to my family."

"Do you think it would freak her out?"

"I think her relationship experience has made her cautious."

"Isn't that the very definition of relationship experience?" Haylee wondered.

"How would you know?" Devin teased.

"You're right," she admitted. "I completely lucked out when I fell in love with your brother—or fell into bed with him then fell in love with him."

She wasn't the only one who'd lucked out.

Looking at the life Trevor had made with his wife and babies, it seemed to Devin that his brother had hit the jackpot. And as happy as he was for Trevor and Haylee, Devin was a little bit envious, too.

His brother had never been without a woman if he

wanted one, and after meeting Haylee, she was the only one Trevor wanted. Two years earlier, Devin couldn't have imagined his brother as a husband and father. Now he was both, and he'd never been happier.

Of course, Devin was pretty happy, too, because he had an amazing sister-in-law and the cutest niece and nephew in the history of the world. And that was definitely not an exaggeration!

Would he ever be lucky enough to find the same kind of happiness that Trevor had found with Haylee?

He'd never been sure that marriage was in the cards for him. Probably because he'd never believed he'd be lucky enough to find a woman willing to put up with what his family referred to as his personality quirks.

Being with Claire—knowing that she wanted to be with him—gave him hope that he might have been wrong.

Claire was stark naked in her bedroom upstairs when she heard the screen door open—and close—downstairs.

"Some guard dog you are," she muttered to Ed, who was sleeping on his doggy bed beneath the window.

He opened one eye and offered up a soft "woof."

"Too little, too late," she told him, hastily wiggling into her panties as she glanced at the clock beside her bed.

"You're early," she called out.

And though she was surprised that Devin would walk right into the house, it was possible that she hadn't heard him knocking because she'd been drying her hair.

But what was Ed's excuse? Wasn't it his job to alert her to visitors?

Of course, it was possible that he'd become so accustomed to Devin coming and going that he didn't think his presence needed to be announced.

"And here I thought I was right on time."

Not Devin's voice.

Sarah's.

Claire was always happy to see her friend, but Sarah's surprise appearance today made her feel a little uneasy.

She'd spent a fair bit of time thinking about Devin's train-of-thought analogy and decided that it probably applied to most people, with some people simply being able to switch between tracks more easily than others. Claire would have said that she was one of those people, but right now, she was struggling a little bit, trying to imagine why her friend was here while shoving her arms into a robe to cover up the silky lace underwear she'd put on in the hopes that her friend's cousin might later take it off her.

The sound of footsteps on the stairs finally roused Ed from his bed, and he went to investigate.

"Hello, Eduardo." Sarah greeted the dog by scratching behind both ears, and he responded with a blissful sigh.

"Why is it that everyone greets the dog before they greet me?" Claire wondered aloud.

"I'm not sure who *everyone* is, but I do it because I like him better," Sarah responded teasingly.

"Did you come here to see him or me?"

"Both." Perfectly at home in her friend's home, Sarah stretched out on the bed and patted the mattress beside her.

Ed immediately hopped up in response to the wordless invitation.

Claire sighed. "He's not supposed to be up on the bed."

"Why not? By your own admission, no one else uses the space," her friend teased. "Although the scene in the dining room downstairs suggests that you're hoping to change that."

Of course Sarah would have noticed that the table was set for two.

"It's just dinner."

"Uh-huh." Her friend's gaze narrowed. "Did you shave your legs?"

"Are you here on behalf of the grooming police?"

"A-ha! You *did* shave your legs," Sarah decided. "Proof that you're planning to tangle them with another set of legs."

"I'm not *planning* any such thing," she denied. "But I wouldn't necessarily object if things spontaneously moved in that direction."

"You need to look up the word *spontaneous*, because candles on the table, ready to be lit, and wine glasses, waiting to be filled, do *not* suggest spontaneity."

"Well, I have plans for dinner, obviously."

"With whom? Because the last time we talked, you didn't mention that you were seeing anyone."

"Because I wasn't. I'm not."

"Candles and wine," Sarah said again.

Claire hesitated.

"And that nibbling-your-lower-lip thing is what you do when you don't want to tell me something."

She pulled her teeth back into her mouth.

"It's Devin," she finally confided.

"Obviously there's been some progress in your relationship since we last spoke."

"Some," she agreed.

Sarah studied her for a long moment. "*Damn*, you really like him, don't you?"

"You're the one who set us up," Claire reminded her friend. "Why do you now sound worried?"

"Because I didn't expect you to develop deep feelings for him… I just thought it was time for you to get back on the horse, so to speak."

"But now you think he's going to break my heart," she realized.

"No," Sarah immediately denied. Then she sighed. "Not on purpose, anyway. Devin is probably the sweetest guy I know. He'd never intentionally hurt anyone, but he can sometimes be a little…clueless…when it comes to other people's feelings."

"He is sweet," Claire agreed. "And smart and sexy. And when he kisses me—"

"You can stop there. Please."

"That's the problem—we have stopped there. All we've shared are a few kisses that leave me wanting so much more."

"I don't need the details," Sarah said.

"But you need something," she realized.

"What do you mean?"

"You never stop by without a reason. You're always welcome," Claire was quick to reassure her friend. "But just dropping by is very out of character for you. What's going on?"

Sarah opened her mouth to say something, then closed it again and shook her head.

"Why aren't you talking?"

"Because it's not important." Sarah slid off the bed and turned her attention to straightening the covers she'd rumpled.

Claire recognized the busyness as one of her friend's avoidance techniques.

"Important enough for you to drive out here to see me," she noted.

"Maybe," she acknowledged. "But it's not urgent, and while I'm sure that greeting my cousin at the door in a robe might speed along the seduction part of the evening, your dinner might be ruined, so I'll let you take the time you need to get dressed."

Claire stepped in front of the door, blocking the exit, and took Sarah's hands. "You're my best friend. Whatever you need, I'm here for you. Anytime."

"I know," Sarah said. "And right now, I need to not be in the way of your blossoming romance."

"We'll talk tomorrow, then," she decided. "Breakfast at the diner?"

"Let's say brunch at one o'clock," her friend suggested with a sly smile. "That way, if you want to sleep in—or lounge in bed for other reasons—you can do just that."

"Brunch tomorrow sounds good," she agreed.

Sarah gave her a quick hug, patted Ed on the head and hurried off, leaving Claire to focus on dinner—and Devin—tonight.

Chapter Twelve

Though it had been a long time since he'd gone on a date—and he wasn't entirely sure this was a date—Devin didn't want to show up at Claire's empty-handed. The books he'd read and movies he'd watched all seemed to suggest that women liked flowers.

But what kind of flowers?

Roses were bold, carnations were bland and a pre-mixed bouquet just seemed lazy. After wandering around Blossom's Flower Shop for fifteen minutes—and wishing he'd thought to ask Haylee's advice on the subject of flowers—he finally settled on orange and yellow gerberas, because they were bright and sunny and they seemed like something that would appeal to Claire.

When he finally pulled into the driveway at Twilight Valley—after sitting parked at the side of the road for ten minutes because he didn't want to show up too early and reveal how eager he was—he chuckled to see Ed racing around, pretending to chase the goats. The dog abandoned his pursuit quickly enough when he recognized the SUV, then pranced around on his back legs when Devin emerged from the vehicle, trying to sniff the bouquet of flowers.

"Sorry, buddy. Those aren't for you." He pulled a dog treat out of his pocket. "But this is."

Ed plopped down on his butt, and Devin gave him the snack.

"You're going to spoil his dinner," Claire admonished.

Devin looked up, an automatic apology on his lips.

The words tumbled back down his throat, sticking there.

He had to swallow around them before he could speak, and when he did, he said, "You're wearing a dress."

"You brought me flowers."

"Huh?"

She smiled. "I thought we were taking turns stating the obvious."

It was his turn again. "You're beautiful."

Her smile widened.

"Seriously, stunningly beautiful," he said.

And it was true.

He'd been struck by her beauty not only on the first day they'd met but every single time he'd been in her presence since then. Whether she was grooming horses or mucking out stalls or crying over a silly, sad dog, she was quite simply the most beautiful woman he'd ever known.

But tonight, she absolutely took his breath away.

The dress she was wearing had tiny little straps, a snug bodice that hugged her breasts in a way he'd only dreamed of doing, and a flowy skirt with a ruffled hem that floated just above her knees. Her legs were bare and on her feet she wore wedge-heeled sandals with narrow straps that tied around her ankles.

When she was in the stables, her hair was inevitably tied out of her way, either in a braid or a ponytail—sometimes two ponytails—and tucked beneath a cowboy hat. Tonight it was unrestrained, and loose honey-colored curls spilled over her shoulders. She'd darkened her eyelashes and the gloss on her lips drew his attention to her mouth, making him yearn to kiss her again right now.

Before he could decide whether or not he was brave enough to do so, she turned to walk back into the house.

He followed.

"Why don't you pour the wine while I put these in some water?" she suggested.

"I can do that," he agreed.

She found a vase and filled it from the tap, then cut the stems of the flowers and arranged them in the glass container. "Gerberas are one of my favorite flowers," she told him. "Thank you for these."

"You're welcome. Thanks for offering to cook—whatever it is, it smells amazing."

"Chicken pancetta linguine with peas and parmesan."

"And sounds fancy," he said.

She laughed. "It's not."

But it looked pretty fancy, too, when she set a plate in front of him.

"You even put green stuff on top like they do in a restaurant," he noted.

"The green stuff is parsley," she told him.

"But what is its purpose?"

"Its purpose is to enhance the presentation, allowing you to taste with your eyes before the food ever touches your tongue."

"Well, according to my eyes, this is delicious."

"Hopefully your taste buds will agree."

"I have no doubt." He picked up his fork. "And again, thank you, sincerely. This is undoubtedly going to be the best meal I've had in…weeks. Maybe months."

"Well, dig in," she said.

He didn't need to be told twice.

While they ate, they chatted easily about the current residents of Twilight Valley and Claire's plan—if she could raise funds—to add an exercise track and cold saltwater spa. She asked about his work, too, and her eyes didn't completely glaze over when he explained his role at Blake Mining or even when he told her about his game design projects, so he took it as a good sign that he hadn't gone into full-nerd mode.

"I was right," he said, setting his fork and knife on his empty plate at the end of the meal. "That was delicious."

"Because the presentation prepared you for something delicious," she said, pushing away from the table to clear the dishes.

"I have no doubt that was part of it," he said, following her to the kitchen with the empty bread basket and salad bowl. "But I think the bigger part was the company."

The hint of color in her cheeks told him that she was pleased by his remark even as she protested his help with the tidying up.

"Why don't you sit and have another glass of wine while I finish up in here?" she suggested.

"I want to help," he said. "And considering that I have to drive home, I probably shouldn't have anything more to drink."

Obviously the man didn't come for dinner with any expectations about spending the night, Claire mused, both grateful and a little frustrated. Sure, it was nice to be with a man who didn't take anything for granted— but she wished he wasn't quite so clueless. Tonight hadn't been sandwiches under fluorescent lights in the kitchen—it had been pasta and wine by candlelight in the dining room. A prelude to seduction.

"And who needs wine, when I can get drunk off your kisses?" he asked, dipping his head to put his mouth on hers.

So maybe he wasn't completely clueless after all, she decided. And when he slid his tongue between her lips, she met it with her own.

His hands were on her hips—she could feel the imprint of their shape, burning like a brand through the thin fabric of her dress. One hand slid up her torso, skimming the side of her breast, making her shiver. Then he hooked a finger in one of the skinny straps on her dress, dragged it over her shoulder and down her arm, baring her breast. He kissed the side of her throat, her collarbone, lower.

Not clueless at all.

Her head fell back on a sigh of pleasure as his lips closed around her nipple. He pulled it into his mouth, laved the peak with his tongue, making her gasp. He repeated the same process with the other dress strap, following the exact same path to the other breast.

His unshaven jaw scraped against her skin as he nuzzled the valley between her breasts, making her shiver. His thumbs stroked over her already taut nipples, shooting arrows of sensation from those turgid peaks to her core.

Her head was spinning as a myriad of glorious sensations assaulted her from all directions, but she wanted to touch him, too. To make him feel at least some of the same pleasure that she was experiencing.

Her hand made its way to the front of his jeans, where the denim was straining to contain the evidence of his arousal. She stroked him through the thick fabric and heard him groan.

But it wasn't enough.

She wanted—*needed*—more.

She fumbled with his belt buckle, her fingers clumsy in their eagerness. But once the belt was undone, she made quick work of the button and carefully eased down the zipper. Then she reached inside and wrapped her fingers around him.

He groaned again, a sound of pleasure that vibrated

through every one of her nerve endings, heightening her own excitement.

It had been more than ten months since she'd been intimate with a man, but at no point during that time had she felt as if she was missing out on anything.

She felt deprived now.

Deprived and desperate for him.

Suddenly Devin grabbed her wrist and pulled her hand away, his breathing ragged. "Claire."

She waited for him to suggest that they move the party of two upstairs. Or maybe he'd hike her skirt up to her waist, lift her up onto the counter and have his way with her right there. Either option worked for her.

The last thing she expected him to say was, "I have to go."

But those were the words that came out of his mouth— and then he was gone.

Claire might have forgotten about her plans to have brunch with Sarah if not for the fact that she'd added the date and time to her calendar and got a reminder thirty minutes ahead of schedule. Considering that it was a twenty-six minute drive from the ranch to Sunnyside Diner, that gave her four minutes to get dressed, brush her teeth and get out of the house with no time to feel sorry for herself.

So she was more than a little surprised to discover that she'd arrived at the restaurant first. In fact, she'd almost finished her first cup of coffee before Sarah settled onto the vinyl seat across from her.

"You're late," she said, because she knew that if she'd

been the one running behind schedule her friend would have been certain to comment.

"I know. I'm sorry." She turned over her cup as the server approached with the coffee pot.

Claire ordered the spinach and Feta omelet with sausage; Sarah surprised her by ordering the same—and adding a side of hash browns.

"Eggs *and* sausage *and* hash browns?" Claire said, after their server had gone.

"I'm just...hungry."

"I'd be hungry, too, if I ate salad for lunch and dinner every day."

"And also... I did something really stupid last night," Sarah confided.

"Tell me," Claire urged, eager to talk about anything other than her own disastrous evening.

"I slept with Zack."

She frowned. "Zack Kruger?"

Her friend nodded.

"I thought he lived in Portland now."

"Seattle," Sarah said. "But he was in town for the weekend, visiting his cousin."

Their conversation paused while the server delivered their meals and refilled their coffee again.

"He called you yesterday," Claire realized. "That's why you came out to the ranch."

Sarah nodded again.

"So why didn't you tell me?" she demanded.

"Because I knew that if you knew, you'd cancel your plans with Devin to stop me from doing something stupid."

"I would have at least tried," Claire agreed.

"And I thought I was strong enough to resist him," Sarah said. "Not to mention that I didn't want to be the reason that you and Devin didn't hook up."

"Well, you weren't and we didn't," Claire said.

"He didn't stay last night?"

She shook her head.

"What happened?"

"We'll get back to me," Claire promised. "Right now I want to know how you ended up naked with the guy who broke your heart—twice."

"Obviously I have no willpower when it comes to Zack."

"I'd say what you need is *won't*-power."

Sarah managed a small smile. "We were just going to have a drink together—a couple of old friends catching up over a glass of wine. Then he reached across the table and touched my hand, and suddenly there was all this electricity crackling in the air. So I invited him back to my place for another glass of wine."

"But instead of the wine you had sex?" Claire guessed.

"We barely made it through the front door before we were shedding our clothes on the way to the bedroom."

"I'm…happy for you?"

Sarah smiled again. "I wasn't sure what to expect. Sure we kept in touch, off and on, through Facebook, but I hadn't seen him in person in more than ten years. And while sex in a borrowed car was fun and exciting, it wasn't very satisfying. But sex with Zack in an actual bed was very, very, very, very, very satisfying."

With each repetition of the word, she illustrated

counting with her fingers, ending with her hand open wide and an even wider smile on her face.

"Really?"

Her friend nodded.

"I'm glad you had a good time."

"I had a very, very, very—"

"I get the picture," Claire interjected. Because while she was happy that her friend was obviously happy, she was still feeling a little out of sorts because her own hopes for the previous evening had been completely dashed.

"But he didn't stick around for very long afterward," Sarah confided now. "And I know he couldn't stay without having to explain to his cousin where he'd spent the night, but maybe he didn't want to stay. Maybe it was a mistake."

"Of course it was a mistake," she said, her tone gentle but firm. "He lives in Portland. You live in Haven."

"Seattle," Sarah reminded her.

Claire waved a hand dismissively. "The point is, long-distance relationships don't work."

"He invited me to visit him in Seattle."

"For a specific date or purpose?" Claire asked. "Or was it a general—hey, if you're ever in Washington, be sure to get in touch so that we can hook up."

Her friend frowned.

Claire sighed. "I'm sorry. I don't mean to be a killjoy. But I do wonder if you had sex with Zack last night because you feel guilty."

"Why should I feel guilty?" Sarah challenged.

But the sudden sharpness in her tone told Claire that

Sarah knew very well why she might feel guilty—and that she did.

"It wasn't your fault," Claire said to her now. "You didn't tell Zack to borrow that car."

"No," Sarah agreed. "But we were both arrested in it—and then I went home with my parents and he want to jail."

"Zack doesn't seem to be holding a grudge."

Sarah's lips curved again. "No, that definitely wasn't what he was holding last night."

"I'm getting dessert and I'm not sharing it with you today," Claire grumbled.

"I'll get my own," Sarah decided. "Because I burned off a lot of calories last night."

"I hate you."

"You love me."

"Okay, I do," she acknowledged. "But if you want to know how many orgasms I've had since we last talked, I'll give you a hint—it's less than one."

"I'm sorry."

"But that's not even the worst part," she confided. "The worst part is that I thought we were having a nice evening. He seemed to enjoy dinner—there were no lags in the conversation. There was a little bit of flirting, a lot of long looks, some seriously hot kisses and then…he left."

"Thanks for dinner, see you around, goodbye?"

"Not those exact words, but…essentially, yes."

"As much as it pains me to admit it, I'm going to need some more details," Sarah said.

"We were well past first base and moving toward

second—or maybe we were between second and third? I can never remember which base is what."

"Second base is mostly upper body, third is hands in pants."

"Well, one of us was stuck between second and third and the other one had rounded third and was looking for the signal to head for home, and then he suddenly pulled away and said he had to go."

"Did you ask him why?"

"Of course not, because that would have sounded just a little too desperate and pathetic."

"Bastard," Sarah said. "And yes, I know he's my cousin and that his parents were legally wed, but that was a total bastard move."

Her friend's immediate and unequivocal support went a long way toward soothing Claire's wounded pride, and she swallowed around the sudden lump in her throat.

"On a more positive note," she said, trying to sound upbeat, "he did at least finish the website."

Chapter Thirteen

Devin made several visits to the animal shelter the following week, because he needed to get out of the house—and out of his own head. And because even if he'd ruined any chance of a relationship with the most amazing woman he'd ever known, the dogs didn't judge him. However, when he returned home Friday afternoon, he found judgment at his door in the form of his cousin Sarah.

"Don't you have a job you should be at?" he asked in lieu of a greeting.

"I'm on lunch."

He glanced at his watch. "It's three o'clock."

"Yeah." She followed him into the house. "Where have you been for the last three hours?"

He went to the kitchen to pour two glasses of water and offered one to Sarah. "The animal shelter."

"Which proves that you have a good heart." She frowned as she sipped her water. "And only makes it more baffling that you could treat Claire so callously."

"Have you checked out her website? I think I did a pretty good job with it."

"I'm not talking about the website and you know it."

"Wasn't that the reason you introduced me to Claire?"

"It was," she agreed, though the guilty flush on her cheeks confirmed that it wasn't the entire reason.

"Then I don't know what you're doing here."

She selected an apple from the bowl on the counter and bit into it. "Trying to figure out why my favorite cousin is ghosting my best friend."

"I'm only your favorite when you want something— and I'm not ghosting her."

"Have you had any communication with her at all since you walked out on her last weekend?"

He winced. "She told you about that?"

"BFFs," she said pointedly. "And I was at the ranch earlier that day, so I know how much she was looking forward to having dinner with you."

"Dinner was…nice."

Sarah chewed another bite of apple, swallowed. "Maybe she is better off with Eduardo, because you're obviously an idiot."

He opened his mouth to remind her that he actually had a genius IQ, then closed it again without saying a word. Because the truth was, when it came to women, he could definitely use some remedial lessons in love.

Not that he had any intention of confessing his lack

of experience to his cousin, but their conversation did make him realize that he owed Claire an explanation.

And then the first part of her statement registered. "Who the hell is Eduardo?"

She rolled her eyes. "The dog."

"His name is Ed."

"Eduardo suits him better," she insisted. "Anyway, at least he's smart enough to know that Claire's the best thing to ever happen to him."

Devin had no response to that, so he remained silent.

"How could you let a woman like her go?" Sarah demanded, clearly not willing to let the subject go.

"You have to have something in order to let it go, and there was never really anything between me and Claire."

Nothing more than a few kisses that the memory of which, even now, made him ache for her.

"I don't believe that's true," she said. "But even if it is, ghosting her is a crappy thing to do."

"I'll talk to her," he promised.

"When?"

"Soon."

"Today? Tomorrow?" she prompted.

He shook his head. "I'm busy this weekend."

"Surely you can spare an hour to make a quick trip out to Twilight Valley."

"Actually, I can't," he said. "I'm on rug rat duty for Trevor and Haylee this weekend."

"You're babysitting Aidan and Ellie? All weekend?"

"Trevor promised that they'd be home by noon on Sunday."

Sarah waited.

He sighed. "So I guess I could go see Claire Sunday afternoon."

"That's sounds like a good plan," she said approvingly.

Claire double-checked the address that Sarah had given her, though she already knew she was in the right place because she recognized Devin's SUV in the driveway.

Maybe she was a fool to want to know what went wrong. And maybe, when she finally got the answers, she wouldn't like what they were. But in the week that had passed since their disastrous dinner date, she was still at a loss to explain why he'd bolted out of her house just when they were starting to move past the PG-rated part of the evening.

She had a theory—a couple of theories, actually—but she needed to *know*.

She raised a finger to push the bell, then curled her fingers into her hand and knocked gently on the door instead. If the twins were napping, she didn't want to be responsible for waking them.

Knowing that Devin would be preoccupied with two fourteen-month-olds had given her pause about coming here. It was possible this wasn't the most appropriate time or place for the conversation she wanted to have with him. On the other hand, as Sarah pointed out, he wouldn't be able to run away.

Claire braced herself to see him again, to feel the flutters in her belly that she always felt when he was around. But when he opened the door with a toddler in each arm, the combination of strong, sexy man and sweet babies was more than any woman should be expected to resist, and everything inside her simply melted.

"Claire." Devin was obviously surprised to see her.

And why wouldn't he be when she'd tracked him down at his brother's house?

Which, now that she was actually here, she realized might seem just a little bit stalkerish, compelling her to blurt out, "Sarah told me that you'd be here."

He opened the door wider. "Then I guess I'd better invite you to come in."

It wasn't the most gracious of invitations, but she took it.

"I've caught you with your hands full—literally," she noted.

"Actually, the twins were doing a pretty good job occupying themselves, but I've learned that their presence tends to hurry annoying salespeople and delivery-people on their way."

He set the toddlers inside a large octagonal enclosure filled with toys.

"Aidan and Ellie, right?"

He nodded.

"They're every bit as adorable as Sarah told me they were."

"You like kids?"

"Sure," she said. "What's not to like?"

"These two are pretty great," he agreed. "But I'd like them better if they'd go down for a nap at the same time.

I only got here last night and I'm exhausted—I don't know how Haylee keeps up with them 24/7."

"I'm sure your brother does his share when he's home."

"Yeah. But now I know why he's always so happy when he shows up at the office in the morning—it's the euphoria of escape."

She smiled at that, then immediately sobered. "I'm confused, Devin."

To his credit, he didn't pretend to misunderstand.

"I'm sorry."

"I don't want an apology. I want an explanation."

Devin looked at Aidan and Ellie playing contentedly with their squishy blocks and thought that now would be a good time for one or both of them to start making a fuss. Unfortunately, his subliminal message didn't get through, because they continued to play and Claire continued to look at him, waiting.

"Can't we just chalk it up to an experiment gone wrong?" he said.

"Maybe *you* can, but *I* can't," she told him. "I'm going to be perfectly honest here and confess that I haven't always made the smartest decisions when it comes to personal relationships. I've dated some guys of questionable character, especially when I was younger. In fact, when I was in high school, my only criteria for saying yes when a boy asked me out was that my parents would disapprove of him."

He wasn't really surprised by this revelation. In his experience, preachers' kids tended to be either rule followers or rule breakers.

"I got a little smarter in college. Probably because I was living away from home and knew that my parents would never meet most of the boys I dated. And by the time I'd graduated from college, I'd had a couple of healthy, adult relationships.

"But I still have trouble trusting my own judgment," she said now. "So I need to know if I was wrong about you or if you changed your mind about me or—"

"I changed my mind," he said, because that seemed to be the best option to end this conversation quickly and relatively painlessly. And even if it was a lie, it was for the greater good—or at least his own self-preservation.

But Claire wasn't prepared to accept his hasty response.

"Or," she continued pointedly, "you were embarrassed about what happened."

He frowned. "What happened when?"

"It's okay," she said, her tone as gentle as her expression. "Premature ejac—"

"Ohmygod," he interrupted. *"That's* what you think happened?"

"I get that this is an awkward topic of conversation, but—"

"Awkward and unnecessary," he said firmly. "Because that's not what happened."

"It's not?"

He scrubbed his hands over his face and exhaled a weary sigh. "No."

But he'd been dangerously close, and he'd known that if she'd continued to stroke him the way she'd been doing, in about two more seconds, he would have shot off like a happy rocket.

"The only problem I have is that being close to you, kissing and touching you, turns me on beyond reason."

"I don't see that as a problem."

And while he really didn't want to be having this conversation with her, he knew that he owed her an explanation.

And an orgasm.

But he figured they should start with the explanation.

"Has it been a long time since you've been with a woman?" she asked in an uncharacteristically tentative tone.

"Longer than you could imagine."

"It's been quite a while for me, too," she told him.

Maybe it had—but he'd bet all of his Blake Mining stock that it hadn't been the entirety of her lifetime.

"Almost ten months, in fact," she said now, confirming his supposition. "So if I came on a little strong, that might be part of the reason."

"You didn't come on too strong," he said. "I was just…unprepared for things to move so fast."

Her smile was wry. "Apparently you and I have different definitions of fast."

"I like you, Claire."

"And yet, you couldn't get away from me fast enough Saturday night."

"Because…I don't have a lot of experience with sex and…I didn't want to disappoint you."

"And you thought that an abrupt disappearing act wouldn't disappoint me?"

"Obviously I wasn't thinking clearly," he acknowledged. A predictable side effect of lack of blood flow to the brain.

"The only thing that would disappoint me would be if you said that you didn't want to be with me," she told him.

And he knew that she meant it.

She was putting her feelings out there, being forthright and honest with him, and he needed to do the same.

"If I said I didn't want you, I'd be lying."

Some of the tension eased from her shoulders. "Then maybe we could try the dinner thing again—and plan for you to stay a little later next time?" she said hopefully.

"I'd like that," he said. "But before we make any definitive plans, there's something you need to know."

"So tell me."

Devin wished it was that easy, but talking about sex had always made him uncomfortable. He blamed his mom for that—for walking into his room when he'd been packing to go away to college, tossing a box of condoms into his suitcase and telling him to use them.

"I don't know what they teach you in sex ed at school," she said, in the same matter-of-fact tone she'd use to discuss the weather forecast. *"So I'm going to give you a quick summary of the basics."*

"Please don't."

Of course, she ignored his request.

"Sex should be with someone you care about, who is capable of consent, and whoever you're with—whether

she's someone you've known for months or only hours—
never, ever have sex without a condom."

"Thank you for that PSA," he responded, refusing to
look at her as he continued to pack, his face burning.

"I realize this is an uncomfortable topic to discuss
with your mother—"

Understatement of the decade.

"—but it's an important one."

"Got it," he said, wishing she would just go away.

"Maybe you already know everything you need to
about protection," she continued, "but in case you
don't, putting on a condom can be a challenge. If you
don't want to be fumbling the first time, you should
practice when you're alone so that you don't mess up
when it matters."

"Can I be alone right now, Mom? Please?"

Finally, she'd left.

At the time, he couldn't imagine any conversation
ever being more awkward than that one with his mother,
but the one he was having right now with Claire came
pretty darn close.

He wasn't *completely* inexperienced. Even the geek
squad—as he and his group of friends had been referred
to in high school—weren't immune to the trials and
tribulations of puberty. Thankfully, there were girls in
the geek squad, too, and occasionally a couple of members would sneak into the supply closet attached to the
computer lab to see what kind of trouble their hormones
might lead them into.

He'd been gifted with a hand job from Lacey Spears
just before his seventeenth birthday. She'd let him do

some exploring below her waist, too, and touching her—actual physical contact with the most intimate female body part—had been almost as exciting as being touched.

He'd left for college only a few months after that—a geek squad of one. Not just younger than most of the other kids but inexperienced and introverted. The first few weeks were a seemingly endless cycle of events and parties, but because Devin wasn't comfortable in a crowd of people he didn't know—and because he'd actually gone to college to get an education—he'd spent most of his nights studying in his dorm.

Second year was much the same as the first, and the third mostly a repeat of the second—until Rain Brennan sat down beside him in Syntax-Based Tools and Compilers class. They hung out together a lot, working on projects and studying for exams. Though Devin's feelings for Rain inevitably began to change and deepen, he opted to ignore them rather than jeopardize their friendship.

It was Rain who made all the first moves, linking their hands when they walked across campus, putting her head on his shoulder when they went to see a movie, straddling his lap when she kissed him. Devin didn't object, because he was totally head over heels for her, and when she told him that she was falling in love with him, he knew that he was already there.

She was his first love and his first heartbreak.

"I told you that I don't have a lot of experience with sex," he said to Claire now. "But what I should have said is that...I don't have any."

She was quiet for a long minute, as if he'd spoken in a foreign language that she had to interpret before she could make sense of the words. "Are you telling me that you've *never* had sex?"

He nodded. "I'm a twenty-eight-year-old virgin."

Claire was stunned.

"But…how is that possible?"

"You're asking how it's possible that I've never had sex?"

Though his tone was matter-of-fact, a red flush was slowly creeping up his neck, a telltale indication that he was flustered.

"I'm confused," she admitted. "Because the way you kissed me and touched me…well, I certainly got the impression that you knew what you were doing."

"I do have some experience with *that* stuff," he confided.

"So maybe I should be asking *why you're still a virgin*," she amended. "Are you morally opposed to sex? Are you saving yourself for marriage?"

"No and no," Devin said, responding to both of her questions.

She exhaled a breath she hadn't realized she was holding.

"It wasn't a conscious choice so much as an unfortunate consequence," he told her.

In retrospect, she could acknowledge there had been signs indicating that he didn't have a ton of experience. But she never would have guessed that he'd *never* been with a woman.

Even now, she wasn't entirely sure she believed it. It almost seemed like the kind of story a guy would make up to lure a woman into his bed, enticing her to be his first. Except that she didn't think Devin was the luring type, nor did he need to be. He was a smart and sexy man—and a Blake—a combination that few women would want to resist.

Still, she felt compelled to ask, "No drunken hookups in college?"

"No hookups, drunk or sober," he told her.

Obviously they'd had very different college experiences. Not that she'd made a habit of hooking up, but she'd dated a few different guys while she was away at school, and dating usually, eventually, led to sharing physical intimacy.

"No girlfriends?"

"One," he admitted. "We dated for a few months in my third year. And I thought, hoped, she'd be the one. In fact, we'd made plans to be together." He scooped up an abandoned rattle and turned it over in his hands, obviously not wanting to look at Claire. "It would have been her first time, too, but at the last minute, she canceled our plans to hang out with her roommate and her roommate's cousin, visiting from out of town.

"I thought maybe she wasn't ready, and I didn't mind if she wanted to wait a little longer. I was disappointed, of course, but we'd both waited so long already that a few more days or weeks didn't seem to matter."

The toy rattled as he turned it in his hands. "What she didn't tell me—not until later—was that the cousin was a drummer and that they were going to a club to listen to his band play. And she certainly didn't give me any indication that she might hook up with him afterward. Because apparently losing her virginity to a guy who bragged that he'd been with more women than he could count was preferable to fumbling through the first time with a guy who didn't have a clue."

"Well, that was a really crappy thing for her to do," Claire said.

Devin nodded. "So I pushed her out of my mind—because what else was I going to do?—and refocused all of my attention on school, determined not to let myself be distracted again. But then suddenly I wasn't an inexperienced college student, I was an inexperienced college graduate, and it seemed even more awkward to explain that I'd never been with a woman.

"And maybe a casual hookup wouldn't require an explanation," he allowed. "But I couldn't imagine being physically intimate with a woman I didn't care about. And I didn't really care about another woman after Rain…until you."

And the way Claire had responded to his kiss, to his touch, almost allowed him to forget that he didn't have a clue about what he was doing. Because when he was with Claire, kissing her and touching her, everything seemed not only natural but right.

It still boggled his mind to realize that she was attracted to him. To consider that she might want to be with him even a fraction as much as he wanted to be with her. And when they'd been making out in her kitchen, when he'd been touching her in ways he hadn't previously allowed himself to imagine she might let him touch her, it had finally occurred to him that *this* could be the night. That she seemed not just willing but eager to take their relationship to the next level.

He'd been eager, too.

Almost desperately so.

"But how could I let myself be with you when I was certain I would only end up disappointing you? Because how could I *not* disappoint you?"

He'd read books and watched movies—coming-of-age dramas and rom-coms and yes, even porn. Because sometimes a guy needed visual aids to figure out the logistics.

And while he desperately wanted to experience and enjoy the physical act, he wasn't solely focused on inserting Tab A into Slot B. He wanted intimacy, too. Not just sex but the cuddling and conversation that followed, like he'd read about in the occasional romance novel pilfered from his mother's collection.

Okay, so he really was a nerd.

But spending time with his brother and sister-in-law, seeing the connection between Trevor and Haylee, extended to and strengthened by their children, made Devin realize that's what he wanted, too.

Eventually, anyway.

At present, though, he was more interested in getting laid.

Or so he'd believed, but recently he'd been less focused on the idea of sex in general and more on the prospect of sex with Claire specifically.

"So now you know," he said. "And it's okay if you've

changed your mind. I understand that this changes everything."

"I haven't changed my mind."

"Are you sure?" he asked, cringing at the hopefulness in his tone.

"No." She looked at him with apology in her eyes. "I'm not sure of anything right now. My head is still reeling."

"I should have said something sooner," he acknowledged. "But it's not a status that I'm particularly comfortable with."

"Why did you think you needed to tell me at all?" she asked curiously. "I mean, you obviously have *some* experience, and the mechanics of sex are pretty simple and straightforward. You could have faked it."

"Probably," he agreed. "But I'm confident that the first time is going to be pretty forgettable—for my partner, anyway. So I thought you should have a headsup, in case that partner is you." He looked at her then, the hint of a smile curving his lips. "Although, while you're trying not to show your dissatisfaction and disappointment, you might also keep in mind that I'm a hard worker and a fast learner."

Claire wouldn't have thought he could make her laugh when they were discussing such a heavy subject, but laugh she did.

"I'll keep that in mind," she promised. "But just so we're on the same page...going forward—do you want to take it slow?"

"Hell, no," Devin said. "If it was up to me, we'd go upstairs right now and get that first time over with."

"I could get on board with that plan, if not for the fact that you'd be neglecting your niece and nephew."

"They'll be fine for the three or four minutes it will take," he assured her.

She laughed again. "You're setting the bar pretty low—is that for you or for me?"

He shrugged and set the rattle back on the floor, then brushed his hands over his thighs. "I just want to be sure you don't have unrealistic expectations."

She leaned forward to place her hands over his, squeezing gently. "I want to be with *you*, Devin. That's the most important thing to me. We can figure out the rest as we go along, okay?"

"Okay," he agreed.

"Now that that's settled—" she released his hands and rose to her feet "—I should get my errands done and get back to the ranch."

He followed her to the door, then pulled her into his arms and brushed a light, lingering kiss over her lips. "I'm glad you stopped by."

"Me, too," she said.

"Do you have any plans for next Friday?"

"I don't know—do I have a date with you?"

"I'd like to take you out," he said.

"What if I said that I'd rather stay in?"

His gaze heated. "I'd offer to bring dinner."

"That sounds like a good plan to me."

Chapter Fourteen

Claire spent a lot of time thinking about Devin's confession. Truthfully, she could barely think about anything else. It couldn't have been easy for him to tell her about his lack of sexual experience, but she almost wished he hadn't. She definitely wished that he'd taken her to bed last weekend, because even if the first time had been quick and disappointing, at least it would be done.

Now that she knew he was a virgin, she couldn't seem to focus on anything except that their first time together was going to be Devin's first time *ever*. An inescapable reality that put a lot of pressure on both of them, and the anticipation was making her more nervous than she'd been when it was her virginity on the line.

After weeks of dancing around the attraction between them, she'd finally accepted that their coming together was inevitable. When she'd invited him for dinner the previous Saturday night, she'd been more than ready to have sex with him. But he was right—his revelation did change everything. And now, doubts were creeping in.

Not about her desire for Devin, but about whether she wanted to be his first and accept the responsibilities that entailed.

Or maybe there weren't any responsibilities.

Maybe she was completely overthinking this.

Maybe being his first didn't need to be a big deal.

She'd never woven any romantic fantasies around her first time. It had been nothing more than a physical act driven by hormones, and while not entirely unpleasant, it hadn't been particularly satisfying, either.

Of course, men were created differently—thank you, God!—and the simple mechanics of the act inevitably carried them toward the desired conclusion. So she felt fairly confident that Devin's first time would be enjoyable for him no matter who he was with. Which begged the question: why hadn't he ever been intimate with a woman?

He was twenty-eight years old, smart and sexy and charming. Sure, he could be a little shy, even awkward, at times, but Claire found his demeanor an appealing contrast to men whose confidence bordered on an arrogance that was frequently unwarranted. She had no doubt that if all Devin wanted was to get laid, he wouldn't have any trouble finding a willing woman to go home with him. But he hadn't done so.

She understood that there were certain expectations

placed upon him by virtue of the fact that he was a Blake. And she didn't doubt that there were a lot of women who might target him because of his name—although Claire would argue that he had a lot more going for him than his membership in Haven's wealthiest family—and that his caution was justified.

On the other hand, he wasn't physically tied to Haven, and it wouldn't have been difficult for him to make a quick trip to another small town—or a big city—where nobody knew his name. But he'd never done so, and that made her wonder if he'd been waiting to meet someone who mattered to him before taking the next step—a prospect that was both sweet and daunting.

Which brought her back full-circle to wondering and worrying that being his first lover would be a BIG DEAL—and she wasn't sure that she wanted that kind of pressure.

But what were the other options?

Send him to Sheri's Ranch in Pahrump to learn the ropes from a pro?

Nope, that wasn't going to happen.

Because while she had a lot of mixed feelings about being his first, there were two things about which she was absolutely certain—that she wanted to be with him and that Friday was too damn far away.

Devin examined the Twilight Valley website on his desktop, his tablet and his phone. On each device, the site loaded quickly and easily. He scrolled across the navigation bar, double-checked all the pages on the drop-down menu and found nothing wrong. But Claire had asked him to take a look at it, claiming that she wasn't able to navigate beyond the home page on her computer.

If that was true, he figured it was a problem with her device or her server or, more likely, user error.

Not that he would tell her that.

Besides, he didn't mind going out to the ranch.

In fact, he was happy to make the trip—and relieved that she'd reached out to him. He'd dumped a lot of stuff on her on the weekend—or maybe only one very big thing—and though they were supposed to get together Friday night, he'd braced himself to receive an email or a text message from her begging off from their plans.

So if she needed tech support, he was happy to provide it.

And if she planned to tell him, in person, that she'd changed her mind, well, he wouldn't be happy but he'd deal with it.

"Hi." She greeted him with a smile and a light kiss.

He exhaled the breath he hadn't realized he was holding. "Hi," he said back.

Ed nudged him with his nose.

Devin chuckled. "Hello to you, too."

He followed Claire into the kitchen, where she usually had her laptop set up on the table, but not tonight.

There were, however, two place settings on the table and an open bottle of wine, two glasses already poured.

She handed him one of the glasses.

Devin generally preferred beer to wine, but when a woman you desperately hoped to see naked one day very soon handed you a glass of wine, you drank the wine.

So he lifted the glass to his lips and sampled the surprisingly pleasant pinot noir.

"It looks like you're planning to bribe your tech support with another home-cooked meal," he remarked.

"You're only partly right," she said.

"Which part?"

"I did make dinner, but I don't really need tech support."

"You're not having a problem with your site?"

"No," she admitted, without a hint of apology in her voice. "In fact, I'm already having some success with it. Several small donations have come in, *and* I've been contacted by a potential investor who owns several casinos in Vegas."

"So you made up a story to get me here for…dinner?"

She smiled then. "I thought dinner would be a good start."

He swallowed another mouthful of wine.

"Are you hungry?"

He nodded.

"Good. I've got a roast pork and root vegetables in the oven."

"You didn't need a ruse to get me to come over—all you had to do was ask."

"But then you might have been preoccupied wondering why I'd invited you to dinner on a Tuesday night—instead, you were preoccupied wondering how technologically challenged I am that I couldn't navigate a simple website."

Her assessment was surprisingly close to the mark.

"I don't think you're technologically challenged."

She laughed. "You're not a very good liar, Devin Blake."

He lifted his glass to his mouth again, so that he wouldn't have to respond.

"Anyway—" she continued, with a glance over her shoulder at the timer on the stove "—dinner has another twenty-two minutes to cook. Should we take our wine outside while we're waiting?"

"No." It might have taken him a minute to put the pieces together, but he thought he had a pretty clear picture now. And it was a picture he wanted.

But there had been enough miscues between them that he wanted to be sure. "Did you invite me here so that you could seduce me?"

She didn't seem surprised by the bluntness of his question, but she didn't give him a direct answer, either. "Do you have an objection to being seduced?"

"No," he said again. A firm and emphatic *no*. "But I thought we had plans for Friday."

"We did. And I'm happy to keep those plans. But it occurred to me that you might spend the whole week thinking about what was supposed to happen on Friday and make it into a bigger deal than it needs to be. Or maybe that was just me," she allowed. "Either way, I thought there might be some benefit in doing as you suggested the other day and just get the first time over with."

"That's what you want—to just get it over with?" He wondered why he felt vaguely insulted to have his own words tossed back at him.

"I want to be with you," she said, ensuring there would be no miscues this time. "But nothing has to happen tonight, if you're not ready. I have no expectations aside from sharing a meal and conversation—and hopefully a few kisses."

He took her wineglass out of her hand and set it with his on the counter.

"Let's start there," he suggested, and drew her into his arms.

And then neither of them said anything else for a long while, because their mouths were fused together in a kiss that was long and slow and deep.

He enjoyed kissing Claire, was certain he could go on kissing her for hours, days, even weeks. But when she lifted her hands to link them behind his head, her fingers slid through his hair, and the brush of her fingertips against his scalp was unexpectedly erotic, incredibly arousing. And suddenly, kissing wasn't nearly enough.

He eased his lips from hers, not because he wanted to stop kissing her, but because he wanted more.

So much more.

He wanted to explore every inch of her naked body with his hands and his lips. He wanted to touch and taste and give her pleasure. He wanted to know—*finally* know—the joy of having his body joined intimately with another, and to find his release inside her.

He wanted everything she was offering, and the wanting made him rock-hard, aching for her.

But tonight, finally, he was going to assuage that ache.

With that promise in mind, he scooped her into his arms.

"What are you doing?" Claire demanded, startled to find herself off her feet and cradled against his chest.

"Getting the first time over with, as you suggested," he said.

"But…I thought you were hungry."

"Starved," he confirmed.

He started up the stairs, Ed at his heels, obviously not wanting to be left out of the fun.

Devin paused at the top of the landing.

"First door on the right," she told him.

The dog raced past them and leaped onto the mattress.

Devin set Claire on her feet beside the bed, then looked at Ed and pointed to the door. "Out."

The dog cocked his head, as if he had no idea what the human was saying to him.

So Devin grabbed Ed's collar and gave it a tug.

The dog let out a heavy sigh, then crawled to the edge of the mattress, hopped down and dutifully exited the room.

Devin closed the door firmly, then turned back to Claire, only noticing now that the covers on her bed had been neatly turned back and that there were candles on each of the night tables that flanked the queen-size bed, a lighter at the ready. The colorful gerbera daisies that he'd brought to her the week before were in a vase on her dresser, the blooms only now starting to droop a little.

She'd set the scene for romance, and he was pleased that she'd gone to the effort but also a little worried that he wouldn't live up to her expectations.

"Do you want me to light the candles?" he asked.

She shook her head. "I only put them out because I

thought it might be dark by the time we made our way upstairs."

"Did I ruin your plans?"

"No." She shook her head. "This is better."

"I think so," he agreed, easing her back onto the mattress.

She smiled. "I can't believe this is finally going to happen."

"Trust me—I've been waiting a lot longer than you have for this minute to arrive."

"Four," she said, teasing. "You promised me four minutes."

"I think I said three *or* four," he reminded her.

"However many you can give me, let's make the most of them," she suggested.

"This would be a lot easier if you were wearing a dress," Devin grumbled, as he fumbled with the tiny buttons that ran down the front of her shirt.

"Yeah, but you blew that chance," she teased. "So this is your penance."

But she took pity on him and, when he'd managed to open the first several fasteners, she sat up and yanked the shirt over her head and tossed it aside, revealing a white lace bra.

"That works," he said, discarding his shirt in the same manner.

Their jeans went next, joining the growing pile of clothes on the floor, leaving Devin clad in black boxer briefs and Claire wearing only scraps of white lace. Then those last barriers were gone, too.

"Too fast?" Claire asked, when she realized that he had gone still.

He shook his head. "Just admiring the view."

She smiled then. "Aren't you a charmer."

"Nope," he said. "I'm just a guy who isn't daring to question how I got here for fear that I'll discover you're a dream."

"I'm not a dream." She took his hand and brought it to her breast. "Can you feel my heart beating?"

He nodded, because he could. But of greater fascination to Devin was the warm softness of her skin. He shifted his hand to cup her breast, stroking his fingers over the peak of her nipple.

She splayed her hand on his chest. "I can feel yours, too."

He wasn't surprised—his heart was hammering so hard and fast, he wondered that it didn't crack his ribs.

"I'm just as real as you are," she said now. "And I want you, Devin. Today. Now."

Her hand slid down his chest, over his abdomen.

Her fingers wrapped around him, making him groan.

She smiled. "I think you're ready."

"More than ready," he confirmed. "But I want to be sure you're ready, too." His fingers sifted through her curls and parted the soft folds of skin at her center to discover that she was indeed wet—and oh, how that realization turned him on.

"Satisfied?" she asked.

"Not even close."

"Let's see what we can do about that." She pushed

him back onto the mattress and straddled his hips with her knees.

He lifted a brow. "You like to be in charge, don't you?"

"Isn't there a saying about letting the partner who knows the music lead the dance?"

"I don't think so."

"Well, there should be," she said, stretching to reach into the drawer of her night table for a condom.

"Actually, I'm pretty sure that the man's always supposed to lead," he told her.

"Then I'll let you lead when we go dancing. But tonight—"

"Tonight," he interrupted, rising up and rolling her over so that their positions were reversed, "is for both of us, and I want to ensure you experience at least some pleasure before I take mine."

"What are you—? Oh."

The last word was more of a sigh as he spread her legs apart and lowered his head between her thighs.

This was a first for him, too, and he was completely winging it here, but his research had indicated it was the quickest and most likely path to a woman's satisfaction. And Claire's pleasure mattered to him. She was the personification of every fantasy that had sustained him over the years, and no way in hell was he going to waste the opportunity that he'd been given.

But his hands were shaking—hell, his whole body was shaking with anticipation—as they parted her slick folds, baring the ultrasensitive bundle of nerves to his hungry gaze and his hungrier mouth.

This part was supposed to be for her, but as Devin began the intimate exploration with his mouth, his own blood began to pulse and pound. He teased and tasted with his lips and his tongue, taking his cues from her throaty moans and breathless whimpers, driving her inexorably toward the verge of climax…then over.

She cried out, and the sound of his name on her lips was the sweetest sound Devin had ever heard. When he was certain that he'd wrung everything out of her that she had to give, he stretched out beside her, unable to hold back the smile that curved his lips when he saw the rosy flush on her cheeks and the dazed look in her eyes.

"That was…" Her voice was scratchy and a little bit stunned. "I didn't expect that."

"Was it okay?"

He hated that he had to ask. Certainly, in the moment, she'd seemed to be enjoying what was happening, but they both knew that he was a total novice here and if she had some direction to give, he'd take it.

"It was…amazing. *You* were amazing. But tonight was supposed to be about you."

"Trust me," he said. "That was for me as much as for you."

"I don't know if I believe that," she said, unfurling her fist to reveal the condom packet that she still held in her hand. "But now that you've thoroughly rocked my world, let's see if I can do the same for you."

She drew him down for a kiss, and somehow managed to roll him onto his back so their positions were reversed again. Then her lips skimmed over his jaw, her teeth nibbled on his ear, her tongue licked down his throat.

"Claire." Her name was a whisper, a prayer.

Her hands roamed over his body, her fingertips tracing the contours of his muscles, nails scraping lightly. She nipped playfully at his shoulder, sprinkled kisses over his chest, and let her tongue trace a path down to his navel.

He halted her progress there, certain that if she went any farther south they'd end up talking about premature ejaculation again.

Thankfully she seemed to understand the battle he was waging to control his body's response to her ministrations.

"Next time?" she asked hopefully.

"Maybe," he said, unwilling to make any promises because the thought of her mouth on him—

Nope.

No way was he letting his mind go there right now.

```
int count = 0;
while (number > 1)
{
number = number / 2;
count++;
}
```

He repeated the code three times, then took the condom from her and carefully opened the packet. She watched with avid interest as he unrolled the latex over his erection, and it turned him on beyond belief to know that this beautiful and amazing woman desired him, maybe as much as he desired her.

When he was fully sheathed, she guided him to her entrance, then tilted her hips to take him inside. Just a fraction of an inch at first, then another fraction more. She was wet, from his mouth and her own pleasure, and the sensation of sliding into that tight, slick tunnel was almost more than he could stand.

```
int count = 0;
while (number > 1)
{
number = number / 2;
count++;
}
```

He clenched his jaw as he frantically recited the code, but the familiar instructions had no meaning. Because for the first time ever, he was inside a woman. And in that moment, nothing else mattered. Nothing else existed outside of their two bodies joined together as one.

For a lot of years, his virginity had felt like it was an albatross around his neck—uncomfortable and burdensome. But now that his body was intimately connected to another—he didn't feel as if he'd tossed aside something unwanted but as if he'd captured something precious.

Was it simply the indescribable pleasure of finally being with a woman that made him feel that way? Or—as he was beginning to suspect—was it that the woman was Claire?

He didn't have long to ponder those questions before she began to move, sliding her hips forward and back, taking him deep and pulling away. The rhythmic friction was almost more than he could stand. He held his breath until his lungs ached with the effort of resisting the urge to piston his hips and drive toward the release that was already too close. Because he wanted it to be good for her, too. Or at least not completely forgettable.

So he tightened his grip on the rapidly fraying reins of his self-control and slid his hands over her taut quad muscles to the apex of her thighs where their bodies were joined together. He found the center of her pleasure and rubbed gentle circles with his thumb, watching her face to gauge her reaction.

She moaned with pleasure as he stroked her, and that sound was all it took to obliterate any illusion of control. He thrust his pelvis upward, pushing himself deeper inside her.

Again and again.

Faster.

Harder.

She didn't protest his taking the lead but matched his rhythm, as if racing him to the peak of pleasure.

It was close…he knew it was close. And then it was there… He felt her muscles clench around him, then the pulsing waves of her release, and he could hold back his own no longer.

Like a star collapsing in on itself, everything inside of him seemed to draw inward, and then explode into shards of blinding light.

Claire fell on top of him, boneless, breathless.

He had a pretty good idea how she felt—he was both exhausted and exhilarated—and already wondering when they might do it again.

Chapter Fifteen

"Best four minutes of my life," Claire murmured against his throat.

Devin chuckled softly and stroked a hand down her back. "Mine, too."

"You obviously did some research."

"It's the one thing I've always been good at."

"I think, after tonight, you can add a couple more things to that list." She tipped her head back to look at him then, her expression serious. "Thank you."

"You're welcome?"

"You don't know why I'm thanking you, do you?"

"For the orgasms?"

"I'm grateful for those, too," she assured him. "But I'm even more grateful that you trusted me...with the truth about your virginity and with your very sexy body."

"Well, I'm not a virgin anymore," he pointed out. "So thank *you*. As for my body, I'm happy to trust you with that anytime—and again and again."

She chuckled softly. "You should pace yourself, cowboy. Your body isn't used to the kind of workout it just had—you need to rest and recuperate so you don't pull a muscle."

"Another school of thought is that a body unaccustomed to working out needs extra training to build up strength and endurance."

"Well, maybe *I* don't want to pull a muscle," she said.

He rolled her over and positioned himself above her. "Here's an idea—you just lie back this time and let me do all the heavy lifting."

"We can try it your way *after* dinner," she said. "Can't you hear the oven timer buzzing?"

"I thought what I was hearing was buzzing in my brain from lack of blood flow."

But no, it was indeed the oven timer.

So they got dressed again and headed back downstairs—nearly tripping over the dog, who'd positioned himself right outside the bedroom door, clearly pouting because he'd been excluded from play time.

"Not sorry, buddy," Devin said.

Ed sent him a baleful look and stayed right where he was—but only until he heard kibble being poured into his bowl, then he deigned to join them in the kitchen.

Claire and Devin had dinner together, and they drank some more wine, then they went upstairs again and lit the candles.

Devin hadn't been kidding when he told Claire that

he was a fast learner. He was also an eager student, and he spent the better part of the night studying her body, so that by the time the first rays of sun pushed over the horizon, he seemed to know every inch of it almost better than she did.

She had absolutely no regrets about their all-night study session—not until her alarm went off the next morning.

She slapped a hand on the clock to silence the beeping and began to inch toward the edge of the mattress.

Devin's arm tightened around her, impeding her progress.

"Don't go." He mumbled the words close to her ear.

"I have things to do."

"Is one of those things me?" he asked, somehow managing to sound hopeful despite being more asleep than awake.

"Not this morning," she said, only a little regretfully.

Because she might not have pulled a muscle during their marathon lovemaking session, but every single muscle in her body ached.

"I have to get down to the stables to make sure everything's ready for Trixie." She didn't anticipate any problems with the new addition to her stable, because Trixie wasn't a rescue but a boarder.

Claire had been hesitant when Gael Hernandez reached out to propose the arrangement, because she didn't have a lot of space and there were a lot of horses who needed the services she provided. Gael was selling his property but he didn't want to sell Trixie, and he'd been referred to Twilight Valley by Mick Cartwright.

He'd offered to not only pay a premium rate for Claire to shelter and care for his mare, but to match the monthly fee for her services in a donation to Twilight Valley.

It was an offer she couldn't refuse.

"Five minutes," Devin said now. "Just let me hold you five minutes longer."

Her heart swelled in response to his words.

Dammit.

She snuggled back against him. "I can give you five minutes."

"I'll take it."

Of course, five minutes snuggled up with Devin resulted in Claire falling back to sleep and only waking up again when Ed started barking because there was a horse trailer pulling into the driveway.

She hurriedly threw on some clothes, brushed her teeth, pulled her hair back into a ponytail and went out to meet her new boarder.

When she returned to the house after ensuring that Trixie was settled and comfortable, she followed the scents of bacon and coffee into the kitchen where she found Devin making breakfast.

His hair was still damp from the shower he'd obviously taken, his jaw unshaven, his feet bare. He was wearing the same T-shirt and jeans he'd had on the day before, and somehow he still managed to look like the best thing she'd ever seen.

Seriously, how was it possible that the man had, until last night, been a virgin? What was wrong with all the women who'd gone to college with him at—

"Where did you go to college?"

He glanced up from the frying pan. "Sorry?"

"I just realized that I don't know where you went to college."

"Stanford." He scooped the bacon out of the pan and set it aside. "How do you like your eggs—fried or scrambled?"

"Scrambled."

He added a splash of milk to the eggs he'd already broken into the bowl and picked up the whisk.

She was still baffled by the offhand nature of his response, as if it wasn't a big deal that he'd attended one of the world's leading teaching and research institutions. As if anyone could get into Stanford.

"I went to UT Austin."

He nodded. "I know—same as Sarah."

It was a good business school, but even more important to Claire when she'd accepted the offer of admission was that it was fifteen hundred miles from Haven.

"Did you learn to cook at Stanford?"

"Frying bacon and scrambling eggs isn't cooking."

"You also toasted bread."

"Truly an accomplishment worthy of a Michelin star."

She poured herself a mug of coffee from the carafe on the counter, added a generous dollop of milk.

"What do you know about Michelin stars?" she asked curiously.

"Aren't they part of the Alpha Centauri system?" he deadpanned.

"Apparently nothing," she decided, lifting her mug to her lips.

"Michelin stars are a restaurant-rating system introduced by the Michelin brothers who distributed a free guide of maps and travel tips, including information on where to find lodging, restaurants and gas stations. The purpose of the guide was to show people all the places they could travel in an automobile, to encourage them to buy automobiles and, of course, Michelin tires."

She was suitably impressed. "You really *do* know everything."

"Hardly," he scoffed. Then his lips curved, just a little. "But I think I made progress filling some gaps in my knowledge last night."

"Is that what you're calling it—filling gaps?"

She hid her smile behind her mug as she watched the now familiar flush creep up his neck. It was endearing, really, that after everything they'd done, sexual innuendos could still make him blush.

"You know that's not what I meant," he said, as he began to plate their breakfast.

"So you weren't talking about sex?"

"You're deliberately trying to fluster me, aren't you?"

"Maybe." She snagged a slice of bacon from the plate, nipped off the end. "But only because you're cute when you're flustered."

"Cute?" he echoed with a frown.

"Absolutely adorable," she said, accepting the plate of eggs, bacon and toast that he offered.

His scowl deepened. "Eat your eggs before they get cold."

"That wasn't meant to be an insult," she assured him, picking up her fork.

"Maybe not," he allowed. "But it sounded like you were describing a cuddly toy, not the man who made you come countless times last night."

It was a valiant effort at dirty talk, but once again, that telltale flush gave him away.

"I'll bet you did count," she said.

"Maybe."

And there was that hint of a smile again—absolutely adorable.

"Then you should feel pretty confident in your ability to pleasure a woman."

His smile widened a little. "Or at least one woman. And that's all that matters, because she's the only one I want."

Claire didn't doubt that he meant the words. That right now, in this moment, he was perfectly content to be with her.

But she also knew that this was only a moment. And while she was hopeful that there would be a lot more moments with Devin before he moved on, she knew that he would move on. Because eventually he'd remember that he was a twenty-eight-year-old man who'd only ever been with one woman and there were a lot of women out there.

But she managed to push those concerns out of her mind—at least for now—when he leaned across the table to brush his lips over hers.

He tasted of coffee with just a hint of mint.

She pulled back, frowning a little. "Did you use my toothbrush?"

"Is that a problem?"

"I'm not sure."

"Honey, we shared a lot of things last night—and into the early hours of morning—much more intimate than a toothbrush."

He was right, of course. But still...

"Have you really never let anyone borrow your toothbrush before?"

"Never," she confirmed.

"Then I guess I was your first, too," he said, with a wink.

"I guess you were," she agreed. "But I'm still not sure how I feel about the toothbrush-sharing thing."

"Next time I'll bring my own."

"Would that next time be...tonight?" she asked.

"Are you inviting me to come back tonight?"

"If you don't have anything else on your schedule."

"Nothing more important than you," he told her.

"Then yes, I'm inviting you to come back tonight."

"I'll bring dinner."

In addition to his toothbrush, Devin brought baking potatoes, steaks and a six-pack of beer when he returned to the ranch Wednesday night. He and Claire prepared dinner together, enjoyed a leisurely meal and tidied up afterward with the easy rhythm of a couple who'd known one another for years rather than just weeks. When the dishes were put away, they sat out on the porch and talked for a long time while the sun sank in the sky, then they went inside and made love until it started to rise again.

The next day, Claire was almost relieved when Devin had to leave early to go into the office. She needed time to think without her head clouded by his presence, because after only two nights, she was in danger of thinking this was something more than two consenting adults enjoying one another's company.

She hadn't been innocent when she'd taken Devin to her bed, but no other man had ever touched her the way he'd touched her. No other man had made her feel the things she'd felt when she was in his arms. Nothing she'd experienced had prepared her for the intensity of her desire for Devin—and only Devin.

It worried her—more than a little. Because she didn't have a great track record when it came to relationships. Because it was all fun and games until someone fell in love—and she was usually that someone. The same someone who inevitably ended up with a broken heart.

When Devin got home from the office late Thursday morning, he saw a message pop up on the side of his screen.

Everything OK?

It was from Briggs, a member of his online gaming group that also included RJ, Sprocket and Laura.

Sure. Why?

Because it's Thursday.

And Thursday was the day after Wednesday—and every Wednesday night for the past three years, they'd participated in an online *League of Legends* game.

Every Wednesday except the night before, when he'd been so wrapped up in Claire that he'd completely forgotten about his online friends.

Sorry—something came up.

That's a sad excuse, dude.

I know.

I hope it was a chick. You know that getting laid is the only acceptable excuse for skipping out.

Devin wasn't quite sure how to respond to that. And while this kind of banter between them wasn't really anything new, it felt different now. *He* felt different now. Not because he'd had sex—although hallelujah for that!—but because spending time with Claire over the past few weeks had opened his eyes to the world outside of his own.

Or a dude, if that's more your thing.

I had a date—with a woman.

Because Claire Lamontagne was *not* a chick.

An actual living, breathing human female?

Though Briggs hadn't added a shocked face emoji to the question, it was definitely implied.

Yeah, you should try it some time.

Heartbreakers. All of them.

It was a possibility that Devin had considered. That being with Claire, loving Claire, wasn't going to lead to happily-ever-after. But he wasn't going to let fear of what might or might not happen hold him back from enjoying every minute with her.

So...you get laid?

No, he didn't "get laid." But he did spend the night making love with the woman he loved. Not that he was going to share that information with Briggs.

Since we're not actually still in high school, I'm not going to answer that.

She stiffed you, huh?

That comment was followed by a string of laughing emojis.

Apparently one of us still thinks he *is* in high school.

C'mon, that was funny, dude.

I won't miss next week.

Not very subtle. If you don't want to talk about her, just say so.

I don't want to talk about her.

Which makes me think that maybe she's someone I know...

Unlikely. She didn't hang with our crowd at Westmount.

Too late, he realized his error. But removing his message at this point wouldn't serve any purpose.

Of course, Briggs pounced on his slip right away.

So she was at Westmount while we were there.

Yes.

You might as well give up her name because you know I'll go through our old yearbooks and ask about every girl who was there when we were.

Devin didn't doubt it was true, and though he knew he didn't have to respond to his friend's inquires, he figured it was easier than trying to ignore the endless string of questions.

Claire Lamontagne.

For real?

For real.

You had a date with the preacher's smokin' hot daughter who gave up her cherry in Jacob Nolan's cherry-red Firebird?

Because Briggs really was enough of an ass to ask that question.

Maybe Devin had heard the same rumor, but he'd forgotten. Or at least put it out of his mind. And while he didn't appreciate being reminded now, he wouldn't let it matter.

The past was the past, and in the present, Claire Lamontagne wasn't hooking up with Jacob Nolan—she was hooking up with Devin Blake.

Chapter Sixteen

Over the next few weeks, Claire and Devin spent a lot of time together. And when Devin asked if he could take Ed to visit Joyce, Claire was happy to not only say yes but join them. Shady Pines was an upscale facility, with lots of windows and attentive staff—all of who greeted Ed by name. The dog was obviously happy to visit Joyce, but Claire was pleased to note that he was just as happy to go home with her at the end of the visit.

To Devin's frustration, Claire continued to resist his efforts to take her out on a proper date, insisting that she wanted to keep their relationship just between the two of them for a while longer. Though high school had been a long time ago, she didn't think she'd ever forget how it had felt to be the subject of speculation and gossip, and she wanted to spare him that.

Unable to live up to the examples set by her older brothers, aware that she was a disappointment to her parents, she'd decided that she wouldn't even try. Instead, she'd embraced her reputation as the wild child, and she'd known exactly what she was doing when she'd gone parking with Jacob Nolan: she was going to lose her virginity and it couldn't happen soon enough. She'd scoffed at the idea that it was a gift to be offered only to her future husband. She was sixteen years old and had no intention of getting married anytime soon, but there were all kinds of hormones coursing through her system that demanded...something.

If she was honest with herself, she'd chosen Jacob because she knew he'd brag to his buddies. She wanted people to know that she wasn't Pastor Lamontagne's obedient, innocent daughter.

In retrospect, she probably could have handled some things better, but at sixteen, she hadn't been thinking about the potential long-term consequences of her actions. And though a lot of years had passed since then, Claire knew there were people in town who would always think of her as that girl. And while Devin had given no indication that he was aware of her high school reputation, she knew he'd hear about it if word got out that he was dating the pastor's daughter.

They couldn't keep their relationship a secret forever—and she didn't want to. But for now, she was happier to stay in than go out, to savor every minute alone with him.

Three weeks after their first night together, Devin confided that he had a big project coming up—and that he had a tendency to get caught up in his work and forget about everything and everyone else.

"I'm not going to be upset if you don't call for a few days," Claire assured him.

"You're not?" He sounded dubious.

She smiled. "I enjoy spending time with you, Devin, but I'm pretty confident I can fill my days if you're otherwise occupied."

"And your nights?" he asked.

"I got Ed so I wouldn't be alone at night," she reminded him.

"I can't believe you think you can replace me with a dog."

"How do you think Ed felt when you started sleeping in my bed?" she teased.

He'd actually pouted at that, making her laugh.

"Of course, I'd prefer to sleep with you," she said, in an effort to appease his wounded pride. "But if you've got a project that keeps you working around the clock, I'll survive."

"I prefer sleeping with you, too. Actually, I prefer *not* sleeping with you," he clarified.

Then they'd gone upstairs to her bedroom and spent a lot of time *not* sleeping.

And when Claire was just about to fall asleep in his arms, Devin whispered, "I love you."

She came immediately, fully awake. "What did you say?"

"I said that I love you," he repeated evenly. "Because I do. I love you, Claire."

"You can't love me," she said, trying not to let him

see that those three little words had sent her heart into a complete tailspin. "You don't even know me."

"I do know you," he insisted.

She shook her head. "No. You know the woman I am now. The woman I've become. The one I let people see. But you don't know my history."

"That might be true," he noted. "But it's also true that all the things I don't know are just details from a past that made you who you are right now—the woman I know. The woman I love."

"Devin, I lost my virginity when I was sixteen."

"What does that have to do with anything?" he asked, baffled.

"Once you've had sex, you don't go back to holding hands."

"Who would want to?" he asked, attempting to lighten the mood.

She didn't smile. "I haven't had sex with every guy I've gone out with, but I've had sex with more than a few."

"Okay."

But it wasn't okay—why couldn't he see that?

"Probably a dozen," she told him. "Maybe more."

"Probably…maybe." He pinned her with his gaze. "I think you know exactly how many guys you've slept with."

"Eight," she admitted softly.

Not a dozen.

Definitely not more.

Still, it was eight times the number of women that he'd slept with.

"I've slept with eight different men," she said again. "You've slept with...me."

"Uh-huh."

"That doesn't bother you?" she challenged.

"No."

"I'm not sure I believe you."

"Numbers—and even names—don't matter to me," he told her. "What matters is that you're with me now."

"You only think they don't matter, but they will," she warned. "We'll go into town for ice cream and some guy I knew in high school will come over to say hi and you'll wonder if he's one of those eight."

"Is that why you never want to go into town with me?"

"No," she said, then reconsidered. "Maybe."

"Everyone has a past, Claire."

"Everyone but you."

"Even me," he said. "Just because you're the first woman I've slept with doesn't mean that I was a blank slate."

"You're right," she acknowledged.

"Are you thinking about any of those other guys now?" he asked her.

"Of course not."

"Let's make sure of that," he said.

Then he loved her again, as no one else ever had.

And when she finally fell asleep in his arms, she couldn't imagine ever wanting anyone but Devin.

Claire could count on one hand the number of times that her mother had made the trip out to Twilight Valley, so she was more than a little surprised to see Elsa stepping out of her car when she exited the barn Monday morning. Of course, her mom was dressed immaculately, as always, while Claire was in ripped jeans and an old shirt, pushing a wheelbarrow full of soiled straw and horse manure.

"Should I have called first?" Elsa asked, trying not to wrinkle her nose.

"Only if you expected me to have tea and cookies out."

"I brought cookies."

It was only then that Claire noticed her mom was holding a plate covered in plastic wrap—and that Ed had plunked onto his butt at her feet, showing that he was a good boy in the hopes that he'd be rewarded with one of the treats.

"They're homemade," she said. "Not fancy like the ones from that bakery in town, but the same ones you used to gobble up by the handful when you were little."

Elsa smiled a little, recalling what was obviously a pleasant memory for her. Claire remembered being scolded for scarfing down the rare treats, but she appreciated that her mother was here, that she was making an effort, so she would do the same.

"I'm almost done here," she said. "Why don't you go in and put the kettle on?"

When Claire had finished taking care of the horses, she cleaned herself up as best she could in the barn before joining her mother in the kitchen. There she discovered that Elsa had not only made a pot of tea and set cups and plates and napkins on the table, but she'd also washed the dishes that had been left in the sink: two mugs, two plates and two sets of cutlery.

Claire had made breakfast that morning, and when she cooked, Devin insisted on taking care of the cleanup. But they'd both been running a little bit behind schedule and, as a result, the dishes had been dumped in the sink instead of stacked in the dishwasher.

She braced herself for the inevitable interrogation as she joined her mother at the table, lifting a brow when she saw that Ed was sitting at Elsa's feet, gazing up at her with a look of adoration that Claire had been certain was reserved for his sweet potato treats.

"You didn't give Ed a cookie, did you?"

"Of course not," Elsa said, pouring the tea. "I know dogs aren't supposed to have chocolate."

"Well, you seem to have made fast friends with him somehow," Claire noted.

"I might have given him some belly rubs—and a couple of snacks from the doggy treat canister on the counter."

"That would do it." She accepted the mug of tea with a murmured "Thanks" and reached for a cookie.

"It was a relief to hear that you'd gotten a dog," Elsa said. "I always worried about you out here on your own."

"He's been good company," Claire agreed, breaking off a piece of cookie and popping it into her mouth.

"I'm sure he has."

They made casual conversation for a few minutes while they sipped their tea and nibbled on cookies, all of which should have been perfectly normal but wasn't. Because Elsa didn't just stop by for tea with her daughter.

"So…are you going to tell me what brought you out to the ranch this morning?" Claire finally asked.

"I wanted to meet Ed."

She didn't doubt it was true, but she suspected it wasn't the whole truth.

"And…I was wondering if you'd heard from Eric recently?"

She shook her head, surprised her mother would even ask.

"No," she said. "And I don't expect to, either." And then, as another thought occurred to her—"Have *you* heard from Eric?"

"As a matter of fact, he called last night."

"My ex-fiancé called you?"

Elsa nodded.

"Is this a regular occurrence?" she wondered.

"I don't know that I'd say it's regular, but it's not infrequent."

"What did he want?"

"He wanted us to know that he's met someone."

"Well, good for him," Claire said, and meant it.

She'd hurt Eric when she'd given him back his ring, and she was sorry for it. But she also knew that they both would have been unhappy if they'd gone through with the wedding, because he'd changed from the man who'd asked her to marry him and she couldn't—*wouldn't*—change to be the wife he wanted.

"He's invited us to the wedding—and asked your father to perform the ceremony."

"That's—" *ballsy* "—nice."

Her mother shot her a look, as if she knew her daughter's thoughts didn't quite align with her words.

"He hasn't agreed to do it," Elsa continued. "And he won't, if you're bothered by it."

"I'm not," Claire said.

Or if she was, she'd get over it.

"I'm guessing that you've met someone, too," Elsa said.

Because the evidence was right there in the dish drainer.

"I've been seeing Devin Blake," Claire told her, refusing to feel guilty about the fact that she was having an intimate relationship with a man she cared deeply about.

Elsa might not know who Devin was, but everyone in northern Nevada knew the Blake name.

"Does he make you happy?"

She was taken aback by the question. Her mother had never before given any indication that she was concerned about her happiness. Her reputation, yes—happiness, no.

"Very happy."

"Are we going to get to meet him?" Elsa asked, sounding both hesitant and hopeful.

"Our relationship is still pretty new," Claire hedged.

"Well, whenever you're ready, I hope you'll bring him around," her mom said.

"I will," she agreed, even as she wondered if she'd ever be ready to subject him to her family's scrutiny—or to be subjected to his.

* * *

Claire enjoyed the routines of her life at Twilight Valley. She liked waking up early, feeding the horses, mucking out their stalls, exercising and grooming them and working with them on basic training exercises that would, hopefully, allow them to be adopted by others who would care for them as much as she did.

Being with Devin hadn't disrupted her routines in any meaningful way. Sure, he was sometimes there in the mornings, and when he was, he would often help her with the feeding and the cleaning and whatever else she needed help with. At other times, he'd head into his office at Blake Mining or go back to his own house to do whatever needed to be done. (Because as much as she enjoyed listening to him talk about his work, she still didn't understand exactly what it was that he did—and she suspected that, no matter how many times he tried to explain it, she probably never would.)

But most of the time he'd come back to Twilight Valley later—or invite her to come to him—so that if a day went by without her seeing him, she missed him.

Of course, where Claire went, Ed followed, but Devin didn't seem to mind. In fact, he had a bag of Ed's kibble and a box of the dog's favorite treats in his pantry.

He also had a toothbrush for Claire in his bathroom—though it was still in the package because she had yet to stay overnight, unwilling to be the subject of the next day's hot gossip at The Daily Grind.

He wasn't shy about sharing his feelings. He frequently told her he loved her, but Claire wasn't about to imagine that his feelings would lead to some kind of fairy-tale happily-ever-after. Instead, she was determined to enjoy the time they spent together until one or both of them decided it was time to move on. Maybe her heart would be broken when they parted ways—at the very least it would be bruised—but she'd get over it and move on, just as she'd done each time before.

If her feelings for Devin seemed stronger than anything she'd ever felt for another man, there was nothing to be done about that. No reason to panic.

And though she'd never spent the night at his place, she enjoyed hanging out there—especially after she discovered his secret room. It wasn't really a secret, of course, but she'd dubbed it that because the door was always shut, and it was only after much wheedling—and the employment of other persuasive techniques—that Devin had finally shown her what was inside.

There were the comic books he'd admitted to owning—boxes and boxes of them. Plus floor-to-ceiling shelves filled with collectible action figures, limited edition statues and scale model replica weapons. He also had a life-size suit of Mandalorian armor, a wearable Majora's Mask and even a vintage *Pac-Man* video game console that she could drop quarters into and use the joystick to help the title character evade Inky, Blinky, Pinky and Clyde.

But today she was working rather than playing, using his computer to reply to some emails because she hated typing lengthy messages on her phone.

"I got another email from Sean Noble," Claire called

out to Devin, who was in the living room watching a baseball game on TV.

He muted the sound on the game to facilitate their conversation. "The casino guy?"

"That's the one," she confirmed. "Apparently he's planning a trip to Haven—to visit Twilight Valley."

"Hopefully he'll bring his checkbook."

"Hopefully," she agreed. Then, when a message popped up on the corner of the screen, she asked, "Who's LT98?"

"What?"

"You've got a message from LT98," Claire told him. "I was just wondering who she was."

"Oh. Um, that would be Laura. One of my gaming buddies."

"Well, Laura—who apparently has an aversion to vowels—wants to know if you're available to hook up this weekend."

She sounded more amused than annoyed to discover that the man she was sleeping with was being propositioned by another woman.

"And you're not even a teensy bit worried that I might accept her invitation?" he asked.

She laughed. "No."

"I think I've just been insulted."

"You haven't." Claire abandoned the computer to join him in the living room. She straddled his lap and linked her hands behind his head, blocking his view of the television.

He didn't care.

"I'm not worried because we both know you've never hooked up with her before," she said.

"That's true," he acknowledged.

"So obviously you're not the type of guy to take what a woman's offering just because she's offering it."

"Also true."

"I'm also not worried because we're going to go upstairs now and I'm going to do things to you that are going to make you forget Laura's name."

And then she took him by the hand, led him to the bedroom and did exactly as she'd promised.

Chapter Seventeen

"What the—" Devin jolted as a sixty-pound weight dropped onto the bed.

Beside him, Claire muffled a sleepy giggle. "That would be Ed."

Sure enough, the dog was wiggling his way up the mattress, trying to squeeze between the two humans.

"I thought he wasn't allowed on the bed."

"He's not allowed on *my* bed. Maybe he thinks you have different rules."

"I don't."

"Also, it's thundering."

And in case he'd missed the previous rumble, another one sounded in the distance.

Ed emitted a pitiful whine and shoved his nose under the folded-back covers.

"He doesn't like thunder?" Devin guessed.

"He's terrified of it."

He stroked a hand over the dog's fur, felt him trembling. "You are one strange creature."

"But we love you, anyway," Claire said, linking her fingers with Devin's so they were both cuddling the dog.

Devin tried not to let it bother him that she could so casually remark on her affection for the dog when she had yet to say those three very important words to him. Because he believed in his heart that she did love him, even if she wasn't yet willing to admit it.

So they cuddled with the dog while lightning flashed, thunder boomed and rain pounded on the roof overhead. When the storm finally subsided, Claire gave Ed a gentle nudge and he obediently retreated from the big bed to his own—because yes, Devin had bought a bed for him, too—in the corner.

Only a few minutes later, just when he thought tonight might be the night that Claire stayed, she brushed her lips over his in a sweet, lingering kiss. "I have to go."

"No, you don't," he protested.

"I do," she said, sounding sincerely regretful. "I have too much to do before church in the morning."

"I could come with you and spend the night at your place," he suggested.

"Do you really want to be waking up at seven a.m. on a Sunday morning?"

"If I'm waking up with you, I don't care what time it

is. And I'd be happy to hang out with Ed while you're gone. Or…I could go to church with you."

At that, she went completely, perfectly still.

"We've been together almost five weeks now," he pointed out.

"I know how long it's been."

"And every Sunday, you go to church—"

"Because it's part of my life-before-you routine," she said lightly.

"So why can't it be part of your life-*with*-me routine?" he wondered.

"I just didn't think it was your thing."

"So what if it's not my thing? If it's important to you, it's important to me."

"It's important to my parents," she said. "I go because it makes them happy."

"Why haven't you asked me to go with you?"

"Because the last guy I took to church with me became a convert," she confided.

Now *that* was an interesting revelation.

"Who was the guy?"

"My former fiancé."

"You were engaged?"

Claire nodded. "When I lived in Texas."

Which narrowed it down to a period of eight years. "At the beginning or the end?"

"The end," she said. "I gave Eric back his ring just before I came home."

"What went wrong?"

"I brought him to Haven and introduced him to my parents. Actually, the initial meeting went well enough, but when I balked at their invitation to attend church services on Sunday morning, Eric convinced me that there was no harm in it. He wanted them to like him, to approve of the man I was going to marry.

"And, he confided to me, he was curious, too. Church hadn't been part of his upbringing, so he was interested in observing the rituals, to understand why some people were drawn to participate in organized religion.

"Maybe I was surprised," she continued. "But I told myself to be appreciative of the fact that he was making an effort. Because it *was* harmless—until he decided to seek out a Disciples Church when we returned to Austin and found one that made my dad's conservative views seem progressive.

"There were several red flags that I ignored, because I'd made a promise to him. Then came the big one— when Eric told me that his new pastor believed that wives should submit to their husbands. That's when I said, *Well, I guess it's lucky for me that you're not actually my husband*, and walked out."

"Good for you."

"But I still felt bad about reneging on the promise I'd made to him," she admitted. "It was Sarah who helped me see that the man I agreed to marry no longer existed."

"That cousin of mine is pretty smart sometimes," he noted.

"I don't know what I would have done without her," Claire said honestly. "I actually lived with her for the first few weeks after I got back to town, until I found out that Uncle Mick and Aunt Susan were going to sell their ranch and I came up with my plans for Twilight Valley."

"What is the family connection between the Lamontagnes and the Cartwrights?" he asked her now, eager to move the conversation away from her broken engagement.

"My mom and Aunt Susan are sisters, but I swear, I've never known two women related by blood who were more different from one another. Growing up, whenever my parents sent me to my room for disobeying the rules—which happened a lot—I used to dream about running away to live with Aunt Susan and Uncle Mick.

"Not that my parents were bad parents," she hastened to assure him. "I just never felt as if I fit in to our family. It seemed as if I was always being reminded of all the things I wasn't allowed to do.

"It wasn't like that at the ranch. Instead of telling me what I couldn't do, Aunt Susan showed me what I could do—and encouraged me to try other things, too. To discover myself. And when I told her and Uncle Mick about my plans for a horse rescue—"

"Equine rehabilitation and retirement facility," he interjected.

She smiled. "They never tried to talk me out of it—they only asked how they could help."

"You must miss them, now that they're living in California."

"I do," she confirmed. "But we keep in touch. And honestly, I feel pretty good about the life I'm making for myself here. And though my relationship with my parents is a work in progress, I think we're taking steps in the right direction."

"What time is church tomorrow?"

"Eleven thirty."

"I'll pick you up at eleven."

So they went to church together on Sunday, and then they stopped at Diggers' for lunch before heading back to Twilight Valley to saddle up a couple horses and go for a ride, Ed happily racing alongside, with his tongue hanging out of his mouth and the wind ruffling his fur.

They stopped at the same stream they'd visited the first day, spreading a blanket out on the dry patchy grass—because it was summer in the desert—and watching the clouds dance across the blue sky.

"I can't imagine a more perfect way to spend a day," Claire said.

"Naked," Devin said.

"What?"

"Naked would be a more perfect way to spend the day," he said, leisurely skimming his fingertips down her arm. "Have you ever made love on a blanket under the sky in the middle of the afternoon?"

"Do you really want me to answer that?"

"So the answer is yes," he noted. "Now it's your turn to ask me."

She played along. "Have you ever made love on a blanket under the sky in the middle of the afternoon?"

"Not until today," he said, rolling over so that he was on top of her.

She giggled. "Really? You want to do this now? Here?"

"Anytime, anywhere, when I'm with you."

And so they made love on a blanket under the sky in the middle of the afternoon, while the dog snoozed and the horses grazed.

Afterward, when she was rebuttoning her shirt, he told her again, "I love you, Claire."

She dropped her head against his chest and closed her eyes. "You've got to stop saying that."

"Why?"

Because you'll make me want to believe it's true.

"Because it's more likely that your dopamine levels have been enhanced by the pleasure of having sex on a regular basis, making you believe there's a deeper emotional connection than you're really feeling."

"Now who sounds like the nerd?" he teased.

"I'm just pointing out that physical intimacy is often confused with love."

"I'm not confused, Claire." And he sounded more exasperated than amused now.

"No one ever thinks they are," she told him. "It's only when the relationship doesn't work out that they're able to clearly see the truth of their feelings for what they were."

"You think because I've never had sex with another woman that I'm incapable of knowing my own feelings," he noted, his expression growing shuttered. "So what do you want me to do—have sex with another woman?"

Of course that wasn't what she wanted, but how could she trust that his feelings were real when he'd only ever been with her?

"Maybe you should," she said. "Maybe you should get in touch with your friend Laura and tell her that you'll meet her in San Francisco next weekend."

"If I do that and then come back here and tell you that I love you, will you finally believe me?" he challenged. "Will just one other woman be enough? Or do I have to sleep with three or four—or maybe ten or twelve—to ensure I get a variety of experience?"

"Stop." She abruptly rose to her feet and yanked on her jeans.

"Why are you telling me to stop? Isn't this exactly what you wanted to talk about? Isn't that the only way I can know for sure what I want?" he pressed. "Because that's what you're implying."

She tucked her shirt into her jeans. "I was wrong."

But was she really wrong? Or was it just that she didn't want to imagine him with anyone else? That the thought of his hands on another woman's body—touching another woman the way he touched her, kissing another woman the way he kissed her, loving another woman the way he loved her—made Claire feel actually, physically ill.

"Admit it," Devin said. "You can't stand the thought of me making love with another woman, can you?"

"No," she admitted.

"Because you care too much about me," he continued. "Maybe you even love me, too."

"This is all happening too fast," she protested.

"Apparently you and I have different definitions of fast," he said, quoting the words she'd once spoken to him.

"Sometimes sex creates emotional feelings that get

tangled up with the physical act, and it isn't until later that you realize those feelings weren't real."

"Whose feelings don't you trust?" he asked gently. "Mine? Or your own?"

"Both."

"He really hurt you, didn't he?"

"Who?"

His brows lifted. "I assumed this was about your former fiancé."

"He was only the most recent in a long line of failed relationships," she confided.

"Are you trying to scare me off?"

"I'm trying to be honest."

"That's what I'm trying to do, too," he said. "I get that you have some history that might make you question the depth of my feelings, and that's fair. What's not fair is telling me that my feelings aren't real just because you're afraid to believe in us."

"I'm *not* afraid."

"Honey, you're as terrified of falling in love again as Ed is of thunder."

"Well, if I am, it's because I've been down this road before and I know where it leads."

"You've never been down this road with me," he pointed out. "And I'm not saying that the other guys you were with didn't love you, because I'm sure they did. But I'm even more sure that none of them ever loved you the way I do—because if they did, they never would have let you go."

It was something to think about—and that was what

Claire found herself doing for a long time after Devin had gone.

She wanted to believe that he was right—that his feelings were real and that their relationship would work because they both wanted it to work.

Because they loved one another.

Because she *did* love him, even if she hadn't yet had the courage to admit it out loud.

Four days in Montreal meant four days without Claire—without falling asleep beside her at night or waking up next to her in the morning. But the IT conference in Quebec had long been one of his favorites, and since Devin was scheduled to talk about online security, he could hardly beg off at the eleventh hour.

But after his presentation on day three, he decided that there really wasn't any reason he had to stick around for the final day. So he canceled his last night at the hotel, rebooked his flight and then called Claire to let her know he'd be home Friday instead of Saturday.

Apparently he should have talked to her first, because she had plans with Sarah for Friday night.

"Do you want me to cancel?" she asked.

Yes.

But, of course, he said, "No."

Because they'd agreed that it was important to ensure balance in their lives, to respect one another's outside interests and other relationships.

But perhaps he didn't manage to keep his disappointment out of that single syllable, because she said, "I'll cancel. Sarah will understand."

"No," he said again, because it wasn't fair to expect Claire to change her plans just because he'd changed his. "It's been a busy few days here, so I'm probably going to be exhausted when I get back, anyway."

"Are you sure?"

"I'm sure. Besides, I'll see you on Saturday."

"I'll be counting the hours," she promised.

He knew that he would be, too.

When he arrived back in Haven, he called his sister-in-law.

"What's up?" Haylee asked, after Devin had settled into the empty seat across from her at The Daily Grind.

"I was surprised you didn't ask me that question on the phone."

"The twins are cutting molars and absolutely miserable," she confided. "I was so happy for an excuse to get out of the house that I didn't care why you wanted to meet—but now that my frayed nerves have been soothed by my caramel macchiato, my curiosity is piqued."

"I need your help with something," he confided, dumping sugar into his black coffee.

"Anything," she immediately agreed.

"I have a four o'clock appointment at The Gold Mine...to look at engagement rings."

"Oh." Haylee's eyes got misty. "You're going to ask Claire to marry you?"

He nodded. "I was hoping you could help me pick out a ring."

"I'm happy to help, though I don't think Claire's going to care if it's a solitaire or a cluster or a plastic toy out of a Cracker Jack box—she's only going to care that you're the one asking."

"I hope you're right," he said. "But let's not chance a plastic toy, just in case."

"This is a big moment." Haylee tried to blink away the tears that trembled on her lashes. "And I'm touched that you're trusting me to be part of it."

"Are you sure you're not pregnant again? I seem to recall Trevor mentioning that you were prone to extreme emotions when you were carrying the twins."

"You mean he said I was hormonal and irrational?"

"I don't think those were precisely his words," Devin hedged.

His sister-in-law laughed. "But I bet they're pretty darn close." She brushed an errant tear from her cheek. "I promise you, I'm not pregnant—I'm just really happy to see you so happy."

"I am happy," he said.

"So when are you going to pop the question?"

"She's got plans with Sarah tonight, so…tomorrow."

"Any particular reason you're in a hurry?" Haylee asked, the deliberately casual tone not fooling him for a moment.

"Are you asking me if she's pregnant?"

She shrugged. "You wouldn't be the first Blake to knock up a woman outside of wedlock."

"She's not pregnant," Devin assured her.

Though now that he thought about it, the idea of having a family with Claire, watching her belly grow round with their baby, made his heart swell so much that his chest felt tight.

But first things first.

"The only reason I'm in a hurry is that I can't wait to begin the rest of my life with her."

"Then finish up your coffee and take out your credit card," she said. "Because we're going to buy a big-ass diamond."

Chapter Eighteen

After a successful shopping excursion with his sister-in-law, Devin decided to upgrade his dinner plans from a frozen dinner to fresh pizza. He was on his way to Jo's to pick up his order when he saw Claire waiting for Sarah outside The Stagecoach Inn.

She was wearing a dress—a rare occurrence, he knew, but dinner at The Home Station didn't warrant anything less. It wasn't the same dress she'd worn on what she referred to as *the night of the disastrous dinner date*—this one had a higher neck and longer skirt—but it still showed off her long legs and sexy curves.

He saw her glance at her Fitbit, checking the time and probably hoping that Sarah would be late so that she could give her friend the same lecture about punctuality that Sarah liked to give Claire whenever she was late.

Because she did have a tendency to fall behind schedule, but anyone who knew what her days were like—how many tasks she was juggling at any given time—would cut her some slack with respect to her (more than) occasional tardiness.

And though they'd already agreed to get together on Saturday, Devin didn't think there was any harm in sending Claire a text message inviting her to swing by his place after she parted ways from Sarah. Because four days was a long damn time to be away from the woman he loved.

He'd just pulled his phone out of his pocket when he saw a man approach her. They exchanged a few words, then the man opened the door and gestured for Claire to precede him.

Devin had no idea who the man was, but he obviously wasn't Sarah.

He tucked his phone back into his pocket and walked into Jo's to pick up his pizza, but he was no longer hungry.

Claire had only ever eaten at The Home Station once before. She'd had brunch there with Sarah, during one of her visits to Haven when she was still working and living in Austin. She'd treated her friend, pleased to finally have a good job that allowed her to afford some of life's little luxuries.

As she'd surveyed the menu on that first visit, she'd wondered how many people the local soup kitchen could feed for the cost of a single meal at the restaurant. An unbelievably delicious and decadent meal—accompa-

nied by bottomless mimosas—but still. She'd allevi-
ated at least some of her guilt by writing a check in the
same amount to Helping the Hungry.

She'd never been to the restaurant with a man, though
Devin had offered on more than one occasion to take
her there and she knew it was widely regarded as the
most romantic restaurant in Haven. Which was probably why it felt strange that her first time dining here
with a man wasn't with the one who was sharing her
bed but one she'd only met a few hours earlier.

"I'm glad you were able to take some time for me
tonight," Sean Noble said to Claire, after their drinks
had been delivered to the table.

He'd opted for a glass of top-shelf whiskey, neat;
Claire had requested club soda with a twist of lime.

"You caught me with a break in my schedule," she
said. Because he'd been at the ranch when Sarah had
texted to bail on their plans to have dinner together,
leaving Claire with no legitimate reason to decline his
invitation. "And I'm always happy to talk about the
work we do at Twilight Valley."

Especially to potential donors.

Still, she couldn't deny that she felt just a teensy bit
guilty about being here with Sean. Not only because
she knew that Devin was home from his conference and
she'd missed him unbearably, but also because she'd
gotten the impression that Sean might be interested in
more than simply making a charitable contribution to
Twilight Valley.

Or maybe she was completely misreading him.

Maybe he was just naturally charming and flirtatious

and willing to pay big bucks for a fancy meal at the most exclusive restaurant in town because he really cared about the welfare of neglected and abused animals.

And though she'd much rather be sharing a pizza with Devin than dining on filet mignon with anyone else, she knew that he understood the importance of making lucrative connections for the benefit of Twilight Valley.

So she chatted with Sean while they ate, telling him about her involvement with Storm's Shelter in Texas and her desire to use the ranch she'd loved as a child to help horses in need in Nevada. He appeared genuinely interested in hearing about what she was doing, and she got so caught up in their conversation that it seemed as if they'd only sat down when he was signing the credit card receipt at the end of their meal.

"Is there any chance I could interest you in an after-dinner drink upstairs?" he asked, as they walked out of the restaurant together.

Claire knew that there wasn't a bar upstairs.

The only things upstairs from the main level of the hotel were guest rooms.

Obviously she hadn't misread his cues earlier in the evening, and she was going to ensure he didn't misread her now.

"No chance at all," she told him firmly.

"I've offended you," he realized. "I didn't mean to."

"Because being propositioned by a man I've only just met is supposed to be flattering?"

He shrugged. "To some women it is."

And maybe, if she hadn't been involved with Devin, she might have been flattered by his interest, too.

But she was more than involved with Devin—she was in love with him, and she couldn't ever imagine wanting to be with anyone else.

"I thought you invited me to dinner because you wanted to know more about Twilight Valley," she said now.

"That was part of the reason," he confirmed.

"And the other part?"

"I do a lot of traveling for business, which means I frequently find myself eating alone," he told her. "So when your plans with your friend fell through, it seemed like a rare opportunity to enjoy the company of a beautiful woman along with a good meal."

"It was a good meal," she agreed, willing to give him that much.

"And you did a good job selling me on what you're doing at Twilight Valley, but my checkbook is in my briefcase upstairs." He held up a hand before her hackles could rise again. "I'm not trying to lure you to my room—I'm just asking you to wait here a minute while I get it."

She was both reassured and surprised by his request. "You're going to make a donation to Twilight Valley?"

"I always intended to."

Devin felt like a fool.

He'd been certain that he and Claire were on the same page, but seeing her walk into The Home Station with another man had made him realize they weren't even looking at the same book.

There had been other clues, of course—he'd just refused to see them. Such as the fact that he'd told her—countless times—that he loved her, and she'd never once given the words back to him. Still, he'd been certain that she just needed time to trust his feelings before entrusting him with her own. He hadn't considered that the real reason she'd never told him she loved him was that she didn't.

And *damn*, that sliced through his heart like Sephiroth's Masamune—ending *his* final fantasy.

Ignoring the pizza he'd brought home, he dug into the back of his cupboard for the bottle of JD he kept on hand for guests. He'd never really acquired a taste for whiskey, but he needed something to take the edge off the pain and knew beer wasn't going to do it.

He poured a healthy splash of the dark amber-colored liquid into a glass, then tossed it back. It burned all the way down, but still he poured another.

Yep, he was a fool.

He'd actually bought a ring—a big-ass diamond, per his sister-in-law's recommendation. And the ink with which he'd scrawled his name on the credit card receipt probably hadn't even been dry when she'd been walking into the restaurant with the fancy suit.

He wanted to believe there was an innocent explanation, but when he'd told her that he was coming home early, she told him that she had plans with Sarah.

She'd lied to him.

He was stunned by her deception, devastated by her betrayal.

And how could she possibly think he wouldn't find out?

It wasn't as if she'd been spotted in Elko or Battle Mountain—she'd boldly walked into the fanciest restaurant in Haven.

Obviously she'd wanted him to find out.

Maybe she'd decided that she was ready to move on and figured the easiest way to end things was to be seen with another man.

Just like Rain had done.

But that wasn't an accurate comparison, because he'd never shared with Rain all the things he'd shared with Claire.

And he'd bounced back fairly quickly after Rain, because he'd only given her a small piece of his heart.

But Claire...

He swallowed another mouthful of whiskey.

He loved Claire with everything in his heart and his soul, and he didn't know if he'd recover from her betrayal—or even if he wanted to.

Maybe it would be better to live with this pain forever than to ever risk his heart again.

Claire texted Devin when she left the restaurant, hoping that it wasn't too late to stop by. Partly because she was excited to share her good news, but mostly because she missed him. But he didn't respond to her message, and while that wouldn't ordinarily dissuade her, she knew that he'd been busy at the conference and planned to have an early night.

She had some errands to run in town on Saturday, though, so she left a little earlier to stop by Devin's house first.

He answered the door with bloodshot eyes, wearing rumpled clothes that he'd slept in.

"You look awful," she said, too concerned to mince words. "What's wrong?"

"It's called a hangover," he said bluntly.

She followed him into the living room. There was a pizza box on the table and a bottle of whiskey beside it. "Was your brother here last night?"

"Nope. Just me and Jack Daniels."

There was an unfamiliar edge to his tone that immediately put her on alert.

"I feel as if I'm missing something," she said cautiously.

"Welcome to the club."

"Why don't I make you some coffee?" she suggested. "Or breakfast?"

"I don't want you to make anything," he said. "I want to know why you're here."

She lifted the lid of the pizza box, saw that the pie hadn't been touched. "When was the last time you ate?"

"Why are you here?" he asked again.

"Aside from the fact that I have some good news to share, I wanted to see you. I missed you."

"I have no doubt you managed to occupy yourself while I was away."

"Well, sure," she agreed. "That doesn't mean I didn't miss you."

He didn't respond to that.

He didn't tell her that he'd missed her, too, though he'd claimed that was his reason for skipping out of the conference early.

Had something happened in Montreal?

She knew he'd been working on a project for a Canadian company—had they pulled the plug on it? That would certainly explain why he'd be out of sorts—but why wouldn't he just tell her?

"I saw you at The Home Station last night."

That was an unexpected conversational zig, but she was willing to follow to see where it led.

"Walking into the restaurant," he clarified. "With some guy in a fancy suit."

"Sean Noble," she said, starting to suspect the reason for his mood. "He's part of the syndicate I told you about that owns several casinos in Vegas."

"You told me that you had plans with Sarah."

"I *did* have plans with Sarah—and then Sarah canceled our plans, and Sean was at the ranch when she canceled, so when he invited me to dinner, I had no reason to say no."

"No reason, huh?"

"He was interested in learning more about Twilight Valley, to decide if it was something he wanted to invest in."

"And did you manage to persuade him?"

"As a matter of fact—" She pulled the check out of the side pocket of her purse and held it up for him to see.

"That's a lot of zeros," he noted, with a distinct lack of enthusiasm.

But that was okay, because she was excited enough for both of them. "It's great, isn't it?"

"I guess that depends on what you had to do for the money."

Claire sucked in a breath and took an instinctive step back, shocked by the implication. "What do you think I did?"

"I don't know, do I?" he challenged.

She rubbed her palm against her chest, absently wondering how it was possible that a heart could bleed and beat at the same time.

"You're right," she finally said, struggling to hold her emotions in check. "You don't know what I did last night. But you know *me*. At least, you said you did, and I was actually starting to believe it might be true."

"I thought I did," he agreed, his words devoid of all emotion. "But we've been together for almost two months now, and in all that time, you've never let me take you out for dinner or even to a movie. You've never even spent the night here."

"Because I didn't want to give people reason to talk about us. Because I didn't want to cheapen our relationship by letting it become grist for the rumor mill."

"You never objected to traipsing around town with Jacob Nolan or Bryan Rockell or Grant Anderson," he continued, in the same flat tone.

Tears burned behind her eyes, but she refused to let them fall. "You said that none of the guys I'd been with before you mattered."

"Because I wanted to believe that *we* mattered. But apparently I was good enough to sleep with—and really, you should credit yourself for whatever talents I have in that regard—but not someone you actually want to have a relationship with."

"You're right," she said. "I was the one who wanted to keep our private relationship private. But you didn't seem to mind too much when we stayed in."

"Why would I?" he challenged. "Because staying in usually meant having sex, and I have a lot of celibate years to make up for."

"So that's what you're going to do, huh? Reduce everything we shared to the hours we spent together in bed."

"We had some good times in the shower, too. And the living room and the kitchen, and even the laundry room."

"I get it," she said. "It was just sex."

"I don't know why you sound surprised," he said. "After all, you're the one who told me that I couldn't possibly love you. That I was confusing physical intimacy with love."

"And apparently I was right."

"Apparently you were."

Claire stepped carefully around the shattered pieces of her heart and walked out the door.

And he let her go.

Chapter Nineteen

Devin hadn't slept—really slept—in almost two weeks. Not since the night before he left for Montreal—the last night he'd spent with Claire.

He wasn't unaccustomed to long periods of sleeplessness. In the past, he'd been known to work around the clock when he was in the middle of a big project. But that had always been a choice.

His current status wasn't of his own choosing, though he realized it was of his own making. He stared at the computer screen, not really seeing it, and when the doorbell rang, ignored it more out of habit than anything else.

When it rang a second time, he tapped the screen of his phone to open the security camera app.

Déjà vu.

He shoved his chair away from his desk and practically raced to the door.

"Claire." He stared at her, afraid to blink in case she disappeared, proving to be nothing more than a figment of his imagination.

"Joyce Morales died."

She made the announcement without preamble, and he was so caught up in the fact that she was really there, it took a minute for the meaning of the words to register.

When it finally did, he felt a pang in his heart, confirming that it was still there, and still beating, though he'd been certain it had been ripped out of his chest when she'd walked out on him, leaving only a gaping hole in its wake.

The last time he'd visited Joyce—with Ed and Claire—it had been readily apparent that the old woman's condition was rapidly deteriorating. So while he wasn't surprised by the news, he was still saddened to hear it.

"When?"

"Last night. Nina called me this morning." She recited the facts without any hint of emotion, and he wondered if she truly didn't feel anything to be this close to him now or if she was simply better than he was at burying her feelings deep.

He wished he could respond the same way: just the facts—no emotion. But *damn*, he wanted nothing more than to hold her, to tell her he was sorry, to beg her for another chance.

Instead he said, "Is there going to be a funeral service?"

"A memorial service, after cremation."

"Oh."

"Ed's in the truck," Claire said now. "Nina said that we could take him to the crematorium to say goodbye, but it has to be before four o'clock."

He glanced at his watch, then at the rumpled T-shirt and ratty cargo shorts he was wearing.

"You don't have to come," she hastened to assure him. "I just thought, given that you were most often the one who took Ed to visit Joyce, you might want to."

"I want to," he confirmed. "Can you give me twenty minutes to shower and change?"

She hesitated only briefly, then answered with a brisk nod. "Okay if I let Ed run around your backyard while we're waiting?"

"Of course."

It was all so civilized on the surface, while the emotions churning inside him were anything but. He'd missed her—more than he would have thought possible. And the worst part was that he knew it was his fault. That she really hadn't walked away so much as he'd pushed her.

Twenty minutes later, they were on their way to the crematorium. It wasn't a far drive, for which he was grateful, because Claire didn't make any effort at conversation and he had so much that he wanted to say, he didn't know where to begin. The only sound in the cab of the truck was the occasional, plaintive whine of the dog seated between them, and Devin couldn't help but wonder if Ed instinctively knew about Joyce or if he was picking up on the tension between the two humans in the vehicle.

Claire texted Nina when they arrived, to ensure she'd gotten the okay from the staff to take Ed into the building. Claire stood beside Devin while they waited for Joyce's daughter to come out, so close that he could touch her—if he dared—and yet the distance between them felt enormous. He wished he was brave enough to pull her into his arms, to offer her comfort and maybe take some for himself, but right now wasn't about them—it was for Ed.

Claire passed Ed's leash to Nina, and the dog trotted willingly beside her into the building, with Claire and Devin trailing a few steps behind. When Nina paused at a closed door, Ed whined softly in his throat.

"He knows," Devin said.

Claire could only nod, her own throat too tight for words.

She was sad that Joyce was gone, sorry that Nina had lost her mom, but her heart was breaking for Ed.

They waited in the hallway while Nina led Ed inside to say a final goodbye to the woman who'd taken him in as a puppy and loved and cared for him for the first five years of his life. Unsurprisingly, Nina's cheeks were streaked with tears when she came back out a few minutes later.

"Thank you," she said, her watery gaze encompassing both Claire and Devin. "Not just for bringing Ed here today but for all the visits with my mom over the past several months. I know it meant the world to her to see him—" she managed a wobbly smile "—even if she didn't know who he was."

"It was a pleasure," Devin said.

"I have something for you," Nina suddenly remembered. "I mean for Ed. If you want him to have it. Just—I'll be right back."

She hurried away, ducking into a room reserved for the Morales family and returning a few minutes later with a hand-knitted throw of soft pink wool.

"It was my mom's," Nina explained to Claire. "She called it her TV-watching blanket, and she'd sit on the sofa with the blanket draped over her lap and Ed curled up on the bottom of it, by her feet."

Claire accepted the offering with a murmured "Thanks."

Nina hugged Devin, then Claire, then she dropped to her knees to wrap her arms around Ed, burying her face in his thick fur for a minute. When she'd pulled herself together enough to rejoin her family, Ed nudged his nose against Claire's thigh.

"Ready to go?" she asked.

He responded by turning toward the exit.

"Do you think he's going to be okay?" Claire asked, speaking directly to Devin for the first time since their arrival.

"He's going to be just fine," he assured her. "He had a chance to say goodbye to Joyce and now he's going home with you to the ranch he loves, with a blanket that matches his unicorn."

She managed a small smile. "Thanks for coming with us."

"Of course. Claire—"

But she'd already pushed through the doors and stepped out into the sunshine, pretending she hadn't heard him say her name.

And when she pulled into his driveway, she didn't turn off the ignition, clearly communicating a desire to be on her way again as soon as possible.

So Devin opened the door and stepped out of the truck, then swallowed his pride to turn around and say, "Can you come in for a few minutes so we can talk?"

"I can't." She didn't look at him but kept her gaze fixed straight ahead out the windshield. "I've already been away from the ranch longer than I intended."

He closed the door but continued to talk to her through the open window. "Five minutes, Claire. Please."

She shook her head.

Ed whined, perhaps adding his plea to Devin's.

"Ed wants to stay," he said, playing what he was certain was his trump card.

He was rewarded with a tail wag.

Claire hesitated, then glanced at the dog. "Do you want to stay?"

Ed, taking her words as an invitation, jumped through the open window of the truck and sat on the ground beside Devin.

She swallowed.

"Okay," she said. "Ed can stay."

"Claire—"

"You can drop him off at the ranch later," she said, cutting him off again. "Or tomorrow. Whenever."

Then she shifted into Reverse, backed out of the lane and drove away.

Ed barked, obviously confused and out of sorts as he watched Claire's truck disappear down the road.

Devin dropped his hand to the dog's head, attempting to offer him comfort.

"I'm sorry, buddy. It's my fault she didn't want to stay." He sighed. "It's all my fault."

It wasn't a realization that had come easily to him. He'd wanted to feel justified in his hurt and his anger and frustration. He'd wanted to believe that he'd only lashed out at her because he was the injured party. Because while he'd been shopping for engagement rings, she'd been getting ready for a date with another man.

But once the shock and the hurt—and the hangover—had worn off and he was able to look at the situation more clearly, he could see that he'd been wrong about everything. Maybe he didn't know the whole story, because he hadn't given her a chance to explain, but he knew that she wouldn't do any of what he'd accused her of doing.

Because she would never intentionally hurt him, but in saying the things that he'd said, he'd intentionally hurt her. And he didn't know how to ever make it up to her—or why she'd ever give him a chance to do so

He pondered those questions as he spent the rest of the afternoon hanging out in the backyard with the dog, throwing an old tennis ball for Ed to retrieve.

When they finally went into the house, he poured a bowl of kibble for the dog and rummaged around in the fridge to see if there was anything he wanted to eat.

He found a container of leftovers at the back of the fridge and opened the lid to identify the contents. Garlic parmesan risotto made, of course, by Claire. Which meant that it was at least two weeks old. He snapped the lid onto the container again and shoved it back in the fridge, because even if he couldn't eat it, he wasn't ready to throw it out.

And yeah, he knew exactly how pathetic that was.

Ed finished his dinner and sat at the door, whining.

"You were just outside," he reminded him. "I don't think you have to go out again."

Ed padded away from the door, made his way to Devin's bedroom and came back with a hairbrush that Claire had left on his bedside table.

"You want to be with Claire," Devin realized, taking the offering from the dog and wiping the slobber off the handle. "It's what I want, too. But in the immortal words of the Rolling Stones, 'you can't always get what you want.'"

Ed plopped down on his haunches and barked at Devin.

Actually barked.

Of course he'd heard the dog bark before—Ed barked at all kinds of things, especially unfamiliar people and other animals.

But he'd never before barked at Devin.

"Not a fan of the Rolling Stones?"

Ed just stared at him, head cocked to one side—as if the human was the one who wasn't making sense.

"She's made it pretty clear that she doesn't want to talk to me," he felt compelled to point out.

To. The. Dog.

Ed barked again, clearly not impressed with his excuses.

And maybe the dog had the right idea—maybe if

you wanted something, the only thing to do was go and get it.

In any event, Devin wasn't getting what he wanted sitting at home feeling sorry for himself.

"Okay, Ed. Let's go for a ride."

It had been an emotional day, for so many reasons.

Though part of Claire's grief was a result of Joyce Morales's passing, the biggest part was a result of being with Devin again—but not really being with him.

Someday she thought she might be able to have a civilized conversation with him without her heart breaking all over again, but today was not that day.

She'd gone over and over the events of that fateful night countless times and had finally, reluctantly, acknowledged that Devin might not have been completely out of line to jump to conclusions when he saw her with Sean after she'd told him she was going to be with Sarah. Because if he'd told her that he was going to be hanging out with his brother and then she saw him sitting at Diggers' bar with a woman, she probably wouldn't be in a completely rational frame of mind.

But she would have given him a chance to explain, and she would have believed whatever explanation he gave her. Because love without trust wasn't love at all.

And while she might want to feel hurt that he hadn't trusted her feelings for him, the truth was, she'd never told him what those feelings were.

Devin had shown no hesitation in saying the words. He'd not only told her that he loved her, but that he loved her more than anyone else had ever done.

None of them ever loved you the way I do—because if they did, they never would have let you go.

And those words had filled her with so much hope.

In the end, though, he'd let her go, too. Proving that the words he'd spoken were nothing more than that. Proving that he wasn't any different than any of the other men she'd known.

But Claire was different now.

She'd never loved any other man the way she loved Devin, because saying goodbye to them had never gutted her as completely as saying goodbye to Devin today.

And though she wanted to do nothing so much as she wanted to crawl into bed and cry, she went to the stables instead.

She spent some time with Mystic on the long line. The gelding was making great strides in his training and Claire was confident that he'd be ready for a new home soon.

And isn't that the story of my life? Claire mused. *Opening my home and my heart to animals I know I can't keep—and men who don't want to stay.*

She was walking Mystic back to the stable when she saw Devin's vehicle making its way up the drive.

He'd barely opened the door when Ed tumbled out, barking happily as he raced to greet her.

"You decided to come home, did you?"

"He missed you," Devin said.

She could see that, and the dog's obvious happiness at being home—being with her—began to fill some of the emptiness inside her.

"Thank you for bringing him back."

He nodded. "I missed you, too."

She closed her eyes. "Don't. Please. It's been a really rough day and I can't do this right now."

"It's been a rough twelve days," he said. "And I can't go another day—another *minute*—without telling you how truly and deeply sorry I am."

"What, exactly, are you apologizing for?" she asked. Because apparently they were doing this now, her wishes be damned. "Thinking I would cheat on you or accusing me of prostituting myself?"

He winced. "For letting my own insecurities ruin the best relationship I've ever had and hurt the only woman I've ever really loved."

"You don't love me," she reminded him. "It was just sex."

"It was *never* just sex. I only said that because I wanted you to hurt as much as I was hurting."

"Because you thought I'd cheated on you."

"But I didn't," he said now. "Not really. Not in my head, if I'd taken five minutes to look past my own irrational jealousy to consider that there were numerous more likely explanations for what I was seeing. And never in my heart. Because even when I was certain it had been shattered into a million jagged pieces, there was a piece that continued to beat and believe in you and me.

"But in the moment… I don't know. The whole four days that I was in Montreal, I couldn't stop thinking about you. On the plane, I was thinking about you. Then I saw you, and my heart filled with happiness. And then I saw him, and I just couldn't make any sense of it."

"But somehow me sleeping with another man made sense, because that's who I am, right? Because the girl who slept with Jacob Nolan in high school would surely be willing to do the same for a donation to her favorite charity?"

"No, she wouldn't," Devin said. "Because she's not that girl anymore. Now she's a smart, beautiful, kind, strong, brave, generous, loyal and loving woman. The most amazing woman I've ever known. The woman I will love until the end of time, even if she can't ever forgive me."

And suddenly she was tearing up again, not only because of what he said but the way he said it, the way he was looking at her. As if he believed every word. As if he believed in her.

"She's also a woman who had a lousy track record with relationships...until she fell in love with you."

He tipped her chin up, a hopeful spark in those gold-flecked hazel eyes. "You love me?"

"I love you, Devin. And—"

The rest of the words were lost when he pressed his mouth to hers. In his kiss, she tasted all of the emotion of the past twelve days. It was a kiss of homecoming and hurt, anger and frustration, apology and forgiveness. But most of all, it was a kiss filled with love.

"I love you, Claire."

"I love you, Devin."

He smiled. "I'm never going to get tired of hearing that."

"Good, because I'm never going to stop saying it." She lifted her hands to frame his face, her gaze serious and sincere. "But I also wanted to say that I'm sorry I didn't tell you that my plans with Sarah fell through and that I was having dinner with Sean."

"You have nothing to apologize for."

"Well, at the very least, I should have told Sean that I had a boyfriend, to ensure there wasn't any miscommunication on his end."

"Miscommunication?"

"Very short-lived," she assured him.

And he let it go, because it didn't matter, asking instead, "Is that what I am—your boyfriend?"

"Do you have a problem with the term?"

"I guess it works for now," he said, lowering his head to brush his lips over hers. "But I'm hoping to level up in the not-so-distant future."

Epilogue

Devin Blake hated being interrupted—except when it was Claire Lamontagne doing the interrupting. Over the past several weeks, there had been plenty of interruptions as they each made accommodations and adjustments to merge their lives together, but they were making it work.

In fact, Claire had recently asked him to move in with her—and though Devin already spent more nights in her bed than his own, he'd so far resisted packing up his belongings and hauling them out to the ranch, because he knew her parents wouldn't approve of them shacking up. He couldn't fault Paul and Elsa for their concern—if he ever had a daughter, he was certain he'd be just as protective of her.

But he and Claire weren't talking about having kids

just yet, and there were certain formalities that Devin wanted to take care of before their discussions moved in that direction. But as he looked around at the group of people gathered at Twilight Valley to celebrate the end of summer—his parents, her parents, their respective siblings and their families and, of course, Sarah—he was starting to question the wisdom of his decision to deal with one of those formalities today.

"Having second thoughts?" Haylee asked.

"Can you blame me? There will be a lot of witnesses to my humiliation if she says no."

"She's not going to say no," his sister-in-law promised.

"How can you be so sure?"

"Because she loves you—maybe even as much as you love her."

He knew it was true, and that knowledge eased some of the tightness in his chest. "Still, she might not appreciate a public proposal."

"Family isn't public," she chided gently. "And you've been carrying that ring in your pocket for weeks—don't you think it's time to take it out?"

He'd been carrying it for weeks because his initial plan to propose had been thwarted by his own insecurities. He'd hurt Claire—and nearly lost her forever—by not trusting her feelings for him. But she'd given him another chance, and he wasn't going to blow it again.

Reaching a hand into his pocket now, he rubbed his thumb over the cool metal band as if it was a talisman to steel his resolve.

"Okay," he decided. "I'm going to do it."

Haylee nudged him with her shoulder, prodding him into action, and he started across the yard to the picnic table where Claire was seated across from and chatting with his mom. On the way, he caught her dad's eye, and the pastor winked, a wordless signal of encouragement. Because Devin had visited Paul and Elsa a few days earlier, to share his intentions and seek their permission—which they'd been more than happy to give.

"Claire."

She looked up, a smile on her face that shone brighter than the sun. "Hi."

But that smile turned to a grimace when Ed, curled up at her feet beneath the table, farted audibly.

"Who gave the dog cheese?" Devin demanded, looking around at their assembled guests.

No one would cop to being the culprit, but when Ed farted again, he felt fairly certain that the guilty party wouldn't make the same mistake a second time.

When the smell had dissipated enough that he could lower himself onto the bench beside Claire without gagging, he did so, straddling the seat so that he was facing her.

"What do you need?" she asked, smiling again.

"I need you to say yes."

"Say yes to—" She blinked as the diamond he held up caught the light and flashed fire. "Ohmygod… Are you…"

"Claire Lamontagne, will you marry me?"

Their guests, having sensed that something big was happening, had drawn closer, abandoning their various activities and respective conversations to hold their collective breath along with Devin as he awaited her response.

Thankfully, she didn't make him wait too long.

Her smile widened as she offered her left hand to him. "Level up, cowboy."

His breath whooshed out of his lungs and a happy grin spread across his face as he slid the ring on her finger.

"I'm guessing that's a yes," Lorraine Blake said to her husband, as their son kissed his future wife.

"Seems like a good guess," Elijah agreed.

While Devin and Claire continued to kiss, their guests applauded and Ed ran around in circles, barking happily.

* * * * *

WE HOPE YOU ENJOYED
THIS BOOK FROM

her shop to get a glimpse of her through the picture window. Talk about a glutton for punishment.

She let out a low growl. "You are an infuriating man. Stubborn and callous. I don't even know if you have a heart."

"Funny." He kept his voice steady even as memories flooded him, making his head pound. "That's the rationale Amber gave me for why she cheated with your fiancé. My lack of emotions pushed her into his arms. What was his excuse?"

She looked out at the street for nearly a minute, and Alex wondered if she was even going to answer. He followed her gaze to the park across the street, situated in the center of the town. There were kids at the playground and several families walking dogs on the path that circled the perimeter. Magnolia was the perfect place to raise a family.

If a person had the heart to be that kind of a man—the type who married the woman he loved and set out to be a good husband and father. Alex wasn't cut out for a family, but he liked it in the small coastal town just the same.

"I was too committed to my job," she said suddenly and so quietly he almost missed it.

"Ironic since it was your job that introduced him to Amber."

"Yeah." She made a face. "This is what I'm talking about, Alex. A past I don't want to revisit."

"Then stay away from me, Mariella," he advised. "Because I'm not going anywhere."

"Then maybe I will," she said and walked away.

Don't miss
Wedding Season *by Michelle Major,*
available May 2022 wherever
HQN books and ebooks are sold.

HQNBooks.com

Copyright © 2022 by Michelle Major

PHMMEXP0322

Get 4 FREE REWARDS!

We'll send you 2 FREE Books plus 2 FREE Mystery Gifts.

Both the **Harlequin® Special Edition** and **Harlequin® Heartwarming™** series feature compelling novels filled with stories of love and strength where the bonds of friendship, family and community unite.

YES! Please send me 2 FREE novels from the Harlequin Special Edition or Harlequin Heartwarming series and my 2 FREE gifts (gifts are worth about $10 retail). After receiving them, if I don't wish to receive any more books, I can return the shipping statement marked "cancel." If I don't cancel, I will receive 6 brand-new Harlequin Special Edition books every month and be billed just $4.99 each in the U.S or $5.74 each in Canada, a savings of at least 17% off the cover price or 4 brand-new Harlequin Heartwarming Larger-Print books every month and be billed just $5.74 each in the U.S. or $6.24 each in Canada, a savings of at least 21% off the cover price. It's quite a bargain! Shipping and handling is just 50¢ per book in the U.S. and $1.25 per book in Canada.* I understand that accepting the 2 free books and gifts places me under no obligation to buy anything. I can always return a shipment and cancel at any time. The free books and gifts are mine to keep no matter what I decide.

Choose one: ☐ **Harlequin Special Edition**   ☐ **Harlequin Heartwarming**
                   (235/335 HDN GNMP)   **Larger-Print**
                                                          (161/361 HDN GNPZ)

Name (please print)

Address   Apt. #

City   State/Province   Zip/Postal Code

Email: Please check this box ☐ if you would like to receive newsletters and promotional emails from Harlequin Enterprises ULC and its affiliates. You can unsubscribe anytime.

Mail to the **Harlequin Reader Service:**
IN U.S.A.: P.O. Box 1341, Buffalo, NY 14240-8531
IN CANADA: P.O. Box 603, Fort Erie, Ontario L2A 5X3

Want to try 2 free books from another series? Call 1-800-873-8635 or visit www.ReaderService.com.

*Terms and prices subject to change without notice. Prices do not include sales taxes, which will be charged (if applicable) based on your state or country of residence. Canadian residents will be charged applicable taxes. Offer not valid in Quebec. This offer is limited to one order per household. Books received may not be as shown. Not valid for current subscribers to the Harlequin Special Edition or Harlequin Heartwarming series. All orders subject to approval. Credit or debit balances in a customer's account(s) may be offset by any other outstanding balance owed by or to the customer. Please allow 4 to 6 weeks for delivery. Offer available while quantities last.

Your Privacy—Your information is being collected by Harlequin Enterprises ULC, operating as Harlequin Reader Service. For a complete summary of the information we collect, how we use this information and to whom it is disclosed, please visit our privacy notice located at corporate.harlequin.com/privacy-notice. From time to time we may also exchange your personal information with reputable third parties. If you wish to opt out of this sharing of your personal information, please visit readerservice.com/consumerschoice or call 1-800-873-8635. **Notice to California Residents**—Under California law, you have specific rights to control and access your data. For more information on these rights and how to exercise them, visit corporate.harlequin.com/california-privacy.

HSEHW22